The Bride's House

The Bride's House

DAWN POWELL

STEERFORTH PRESS
SOUTH ROYALTON, VERMONT

First published in 1929 by Brentano's.

This edition of *The Bride's House* is published in
cooperation with the Estate of Dawn Powell.

Introduction Copyright © 1998 by Tim Page

For information about permission to
reproduce selections from this book,
write to: Steerforth Press L.C., P.O. Box 70,
South Royalton, Vermont 05068.

Library of Congress Cataloging-in-Publication Data

Powell, Dawn.
The bride's house / Dawn Powell. — 1st paperback ed.
p. cm.
ISBN 1-883642-78-7 (alk. paper)
I. Title.
PS351.0936B7   1998
813'.52—dc21   98-26161
CIP

Manufactured in the United States of America

FIRST PAPERBACK EDITION

INTRODUCTION

The Bride's House, originally published in 1929, was Dawn Powell's first important novel. It is an uncommonly bleak work by anybody's standards; imagine, if you can, what Theodore Dreiser might have done had he turned his brooding eye to the perennial genre of "romance fiction," and you will have some sense of the drama contained within these pages.

Set in one of Powell's meticulously conjured midwestern towns, *The Bride's House* unfolds in the closing years of the nineteenth century. While the plot seems a little shopworn today—Sophie Truelove, a thwarted and uncommonly self-aware young woman, is hopelessly torn between the safety and kindness offered by her dull, respectable husband and the temptations of a dashing and mysterious stranger—the book is redeemed by the intense and desolate poetry that Powell brought to its best pages.

The twenty-nine-year old Powell wrote *The Bride's House* very quickly, between December 1, 1925 and July 17, 1926. It was her third novel, preceded only by *Whither* (which was finished in 1924, and disowned by its author almost immediately after publication in 1925) and the marginally more successful *She Walks In Beauty* (written in 1925 and finally published, after numerous rejections, by Brentano's in 1928).

The Bride's House, also from Brentano's, was infinitely darker, richer, more disciplined, and more consistent than anything Powell had yet written. If the earlier novels were literally autobiographical, with a clearly delineated "Dawn" figure in each one, *The Bride's House* split the author into four distinct characters across as many generations of a troubled family. Powell's sensibility is at once present in the bright child Vera, the young housewife Sophie, the middle-aged (and once-scandalous) Aunt Lotta, and the ancient grandmother, who has fallen into sleepy senility and yet awakes from her reveries to utter elliptical, sage commentary on the problems of the other characters.

Through Grandmother's cryptic utterances, the rumors and teasing flashes of Aunt Lotta, and the struggles of young Vera, we learn a great deal about what Sophie may have been during her girlhood and what she may likely become as an elderly woman. An inter-generational stream of consciousness pulses through the book: "Sophie is our blood, and we attract suffering," Lotta acknowledges sorrowfully at one point. It was surely no afterthought on Powell's part to dedicate *The Bride's House* to her own aunt, Orpha May Steinbrueck, who raised her from the age of thirteen.

So far as one can tell, the external details of the narrative in *The Bride's House* have little to do with any comparable events in Powell's own life. And yet the book would seem to reveal far more of the author's inner experience than either of her first two novels, especially if one believes (as I do) that it was composed at the peak of the married Powell's romantic involvement with the playwright John Howard Lawson* and that it closely mirrors Powell's own confused mixture of exhilaration and melancholy:

---

*I have examined the evidence for such a reading in *Dawn Powell: A Biography.*

It is a dreadful thing, Sophie thought, for a woman to live with two men, to lie in one man's arms and think of other arms, to smile into Lynn's clear eyes and see other eyes, dark and eager. Dreadful to feel that there is in the world something stronger than oneself, something that might leap out any minute and devour one's peace.

Indeed, *The Bride's House* is a deeply haunted book, perhaps Powell's most solemn novel. Even *Dance Night* has more witticisms, more humorous asides. It was written during what was an altogether awful time in Powell's life: beside her ongoing and profound ambivalence about the simultaneous relationships with her husband and Lawson, she finished the book only 10 days after a protracted death watch over her father, which she endured in the house of her despised stepmother.

Despite it all, *The Bride's House* is persuasive in a manner unlike anything else Powell had yet created. It is charged with a sustained mythic quality—the four principal female characters add up to a kind of Everywoman—and with some splendid realism, too, as in this description of small-town America:

Buggies and wagons lined the street of the self-satisfied little town, flags flew, bands played parading down the street, Civil War veterans marched and a group of youngsters bore a Loyal Temperance Legion banner and sang "Saloons, Saloons, Saloons must go!" But on the contrary saloons had sprung up overnight to meet the county's annual thirst. A fragrant alcoholic haze flung over the town, and tented the entire Fair Grounds. Streets were giddy with laughter and the shrill voices and megaphoned speeches of visiting politicians. There were clusters of starched white and flying ribbons here and there, groups of rosy farm girls giggling and ogling each passing man. By nighttime the groups—with good luck—would be scattered, each girl giggling with an awkward young man in some tree-shaded buggy behind the Fair Grounds, hysterically sipping from a jug of corn whiskey and abandoning herself to private yearnings. The wretched little frame hotels, supported comfortably all year by half a dozen traveling salesmen, now bulged with guests and window shades were drawn night and day, boasting of the iniquity of their bedrooms. Carnival gods rode over the city and sprinkled the orthodox with their confetti.

Powell knew this world by heart and her evocations have the immediacy of great journalism.

The reviews of *The Bride's House* were few, brief, and inadequate; the book sold poorly and it has been now out of print for more than sixty-five years. Indeed, this is probably the author's scarcest title, and I know of only one extant copy with a dust jacket. Even among the several "lost" novels of Dawn Powell, *The Bride's House* stands out for its obscurity.

Still, I believe most readers will agree that it is worth putting up with some hasty writing, purple passages, and improbable situations in order to join Powell on her exploration of a vanished America—and of a timeless human dilemma.

Tim Page
New York City
June 7, 1998

For Orpha May

I

*L*OTTA'S CHILDREN arrived as Lotta had wired they would, on the night train at Ashton Center. They were three gray, horrid-looking little creatures and their names were Lois and Vera and Custer. They were jumping up and down on the lamplit platform in their cherry-colored coats and ermine tam o'shanters—Custer had to wear one, too, though the red tassel was off his—and squealing at the top of their lungs when George arrived with the sleigh.

"We've come to visit!" they shouted to him. "We've come to stay on the farm with Uncle Stephen and Aunt Cecily! Aren't you glad?"

They scrambled across the icy platform and Custer fell down in a snowdrift. He sat there, red and howling, while his sisters kissed their cousin George as they had been told to do and fought over who should get into the sleigh first.

George Truelove fancied himself as a lover of children but Lotta's three inspired in him a bewildered emotion that was certainly not affection. He might have known they would be queer, from all the stories told of his father's sister Lotta. After all, a woman who read stars for a living was bound to be a fantastic mother . . . the way she shipped those children around to all her relatives, for instance. They were bound to be different. Still Dad and Mother had been eager to have the children—on Sophie's account, of course.

"It's lonesome for Sophie, the only girl on the farm," they had said, "and you can't let a girl like Sophie be too much alone. Children ought to keep Sophie from getting moody."

"Rather be lonesome than have these three around," reflected George pessimistically.

"Here, sonny!" he called to the yapping little bundle of red velvet with the lopsided ermine wig. "Better stop crying and jump in here with the girls."

Custer was startled into obedience. George lifted him into the sleigh, aware that the little one was making hideous faces at his two sisters. They squirmed into place and George tucked the blanket around them. He peered across the dark platform to see if anyone else had gotten off the train but it had stopped solely for Lotta's youngsters. In the ghastly light of the station room he could see Tom Hamilton's big hulking form. Probably waiting for the midnight train from the south.

"Want a lift out our way?" George called. There really wasn't room in the sleigh but George felt that anything would be better than being left alone with three children.

The older man swung around, waved an arm.

"Have to wait for the Cincinnati train, Truelove," he called back. "New schoolteacher's coming in and I'm taking her to stay at our place till she gets settled. You heard the old one ran off and got married a while back, I suppose."

George adjusted the robe, flicked the reins and the bays leaped ahead. The village was muffled in snow—it was a solitary candle burning in an attic window yonder, a lantern in a church doorway.

George wished he could have stayed to have a look at the new schoolteacher. You couldn't tell. Maybe—well, Sophie wasn't the only one who got sort of moody sometimes waiting . . . He was conscious suddenly of sharp little knees and elbows and wriggling bodies. He moved uncomfortably.

"There was a man on the train," said the thinnest, slant-eyed one—that was Vera, he guessed: Lois was the oldest of them, nearly eleven—"and he gave me a dollar."

"He didn't!" shrieked Custer.

Lois merely nudged George violently and significantly in the ribs.

"He said," pursued Vera, "'Here, little girl, is a dollar for you to do as you like with. It's a present,' he said."

"That's fine," congratulated George and received another painful nudge in the ribs from Lois.

"Then he said," continued Vera, "'I'd give one to your sister only she isn't as pretty as you are.'"

"She tells lies," Lois hissed in George's ear. "I'm the pretty one and she's the bright one. But she's always telling lies. She told the conductor we lived in the White House. She's a very bad girl and mother and I can't do a thing with her. Just ask her to let you see the dollar."

George was embarrassed. These were the visitors that were to brighten his sister's loneliness on the farm. Hmm . . . Custer was setting up a wail now.

"I want to go to the country," he howled, "I want to go to the country!"

Lois boxed his ears efficiently.

"You are in the country," she scolded. "Now hush up and be a man like Cousin George. He's going to take us to see Cousin Sophie and Grandmother . . . Do you think it's wrong for cousins to marry each other?"

George did not answer. He drew a whip savagely over bush

tops, sent sleeping snow fluttering again into the air.

"Brats," he reflected, "That's what they amount to. Not like Mary Cecily's little Bobby at all. Regular brats. Mother and Sophie are going to have a pretty time with them, you can see that."

The bays had taken the path through the woods and great trees shook snow down over them. The forest darkness became jubilant with sleigh bells, and far away on Doc Gardiner's place a hound barked eerily. The three city children were frightened into long silence. The trees were so black and what were those strange crackling noises? . . .

"I'm afraid of the country," Lois's voice came finally. "I wish I was in Washington."

An owl hooted.

"I'm not afraid," chattered Vera. "Custer is and Lois is but I'm not. Cousins can't marry each other, but I'm not anybody's cousin. I was left in a basket asking people to look out for me because I was really a princess. I'm adopted."

A keyhole of starlight appeared through the trees—the road was about to come out across the open fields. Way off on the hill beyond the frozen creek was the big farmhouse, a dark hulk pierced with pinpoints of lamplight. The bays snorted happily and their heels flew high along the crackling highway, past snow-feathered hedges that defined Truelove fields. Now the house loomed enormous and radiant, spilling its light through fences into geometric patterns on the road.

"Home," said George, and whistled for the collies.

Sophie was drying her hair before the great fireplace in the living room. She sat on a low stool, abstractedly stirring the burning logs from time to time with the poker in her hand. Her black hair clouded her shoulders and rippled to the blue woven rug on the floor. The flames delicately tinted the ivory of her face and sent a drowsy rapture through her body, lulled against her will the unrest she often knew.

The quiet of this room and its contented people stirred her to vague anger. Men smoking, women gently dozing, as if supper and sleep were the ends of all existence. Sophie's fists instinctively clenched, struggling against the insidious peace of this familiar scene. Be happy, the older people seemed to say, because your hair is long and black and soft, because the fragrance of roasted apples is in the air, and because in the dark corner Grandmother Truelove has shriveled into sleep! The old woman sat in a wicker chair warped with heat so that with each breath she rattled like a seed in a dried pomegranate. The echo of her thin voice mingled with the pipe smoke about the beams in the ceiling—she had said the last words spoken aloud in the room, something about Lotta and loneliness and the dangers of washing one's hair too often.

"Let her talk of being lonely," Sophie thought resentfully, "An old woman at least has had things happen to her. She can remember things."

Loneliness, who could know more of that than Sophie? The despair, for example, that she knew on drawing a window curtain to stare out at night storms driving across great fields and forests and to know that she was a part of that and not of the room's quiet; to hear bells chiming in far-off churches for this bridal pair, for that one's funeral and to wish savagely for the torment of either love or death.

Slap-slap of the cards on the table where her father played solitaire. Sophie poked the fire. She could remember when she was very small, sitting on her father's lap while beside her on this very stool her sister Mary Cecily looked into the fire and

George held his grandmother's knitting. What had Mary Cecily seen then in flames? Sophie's lip curled in contempt at any sister's or brother's dreams. A sister married and spoke of confinements. A brother was concerned with horses, collies and town meetings . . . The flames devised a red mask, a goblin finger traced a vanishing inscription on the chimney, the mask shrank and allowed blue fire through its eyeholes . . . Sophie was reminded of the blue-eyed stranger, the man on the post office steps last spring. Somewhere she had seen that man before . . . the memory troubled her . . . but that was not the only reason she wondered about him so often. Their eyes had met that day and then he was gone, but sometimes a stranger's glance could be etched in one's mind and blind a woman to all other men.

Sophie stirred the logs. Now there was a little whirring noise, creaking of antique machinery, the tall clock on the mantel was about to strike. It chimed ten falteringly and sweetly.

"Imagine Lotta sending those children alone on a train," Sophie's mother said, coming in from the kitchen, "Getting into a strange place at almost midnight. I can't imagine what your sister was thinking of, Stephen. But of course that's like Lotta."

Stephen made a soothing cluck-cluck in his throat that meant, "There, there, Cecily! Don't you think about anything that upsets you. We'll just not talk about Lotta." Besides, he was wondering whether to play his trey of diamonds on the four-spot there, or to build with it. That would dispose of the two of clubs there in the right-hand corner.

His wife stood by the table looking at Stephen and then at Sophie and Grandma. How could they be so placid, when something was about to happen? She herself had ached for days just thinking about it. She wanted children about the farm, yes—but Lotta's children—Cecily's fingers tightened on the back of Stephen's chair. A thin wiry little woman, all her life she had worked hard in a sort of still frenzy, and now that the children were grown, she worked even more feverishly to keep from remembering things . . . George's red baby shoes . . . Mary Cecily crying for her at night . . . the twins in their coffin. Work made one forget, though, so Cecily drove herself and did heavy chores that Bessie or the boys should have done. She was very tiny and frail to compress such energy, and there was in her something childlike and incredibly innocent, as if her virginity had never been affected in the bearing of five children. Sophie sometimes thought her mother must be protected from knowing even the dark wonders that were in her own mind; she could not answer when her mother would say worriedly, "I don't like to see you lonesome, Sophie. Why don't you let some of the young men call? A young girl can't be really happy until she is married and safe."

As if all people wanted was to be safe . . . Sophie shook her head slowly.

"I'd better take a warming pan up to their bed," Cecily said. "It is a cold night and it's always cold in that room."

"Let me take it, Mother," said Sophie.

She caught her hair in her two hands and twisted it in a blue-black coil about her head. Reluctantly she got up from the stool and stretched her long fine body. "Like Lotta," Cecily thought unhappily. "Like an animal."

"Isn't it time for them to be here, Mother?"

Cecily rubbed a pane at the window and peered out, one hand resting with nervous impatience on her hip. A log snapped in the fireplace.

Slap-slap—Stephen was dealing his cards again. His beard was wreathed in pipe smoke. Spades and hearts splattered the red tablecloth.

"Don't you go up in that drafty bedroom with your hair damp," Mrs. Truelove admonished, hearing Sophie step toward the door. "I'll take the pan up. They'll want something to eat first anyway. Stephen, I wonder what the children will be like. Dear, I do hope they won't be queer like their mother! I hate to speak out but I am glad Lotta didn't come with them. Aren't you, Sophie?"

Sophie did not look up. It was not right, she knew, for her to feel loyal to her father's sister, to feel this flare of hostility toward her own mother, whenever Lotta's name came up an impulse to say, "You don't know—you don't know. You're a Mills, after all." It was the sort of thing Grandmother Truelove would have said.

"I don't know," Sophie murmured. "I've always wanted to see Aunt Lotta someday."

Stephen hemmed vaguely. He was deliberating whether to take his seven of clubs and cover the eight, or . . . hm . . .

There was a remote tingle of sleigh bells.

"Something to happen," Sophie thought with quickening breath. "Anything—anything!"

"There's the bays now," said Stephen.

Cecily hurried to the kitchen to heat the milk. Stephen pushed his chair and rose, he'd have to help George unhitch. Grandma Truelove waked at the sound of the chair scraping, and blinked somberly at the light. Her eyes were beady and defiant. Her mouth was set in a determination not to grow old; it was a thin, salmon-colored thread in a web of wrinkles.

Sophie moved to the window and looked out. There were snow and stars and lanterns swinging by the stable door and the sound of horses stomping in their stalls and the colt neighing . . . Sophie pressed her warm cheek against the pane. . . . She wanted to lie down in the snow with her long black hair about her and look up at stars all night.

Daylight was always ushered in on the Truelove farm with the sighing and snorting of the pump, and John's "There she is!" when the water finally gushed out was the cue in summertime for the sun to appear behind the barn. Winters the lamp was lit in the kitchen and Bessie, sleepy-eyed and cross, set the coffeepot on the stove and conjured some particularly tart reply for John's inevitable—accompanied by stamping of snow out of his boots and rubbing of his red frozen hands—

"*Well,* Bessie! Up for the day, eh?"

John had been the Truelove's hired man for years. He lived with the two collies in a hut he had built for himself by the creek, but he always ate at the farm. He was a red little man with a respected temperament. For days he would not speak to the family and would mutter vague threats behind their backs. Every night he absorbed a new paperback novel that he peopled with the only persons he knew—the Trueloves. Since the characters were always wicked, John held the Trueloves to account for the wrongs done to the hero. He forgave them only after he had finished the book and the hero had killed all of his enemies. The heroine, always short and plump, bore an amazing resemblance to Bessie, for Bessie, the cook, was John's ideal. Unhappily he was the only man in her world on whom Bessie had bestowed no amorous favor. For John's eternal fidelity she had only contempt.

The pump was frozen this morning and John swore patiently and monotonously as he worked over it. Bessie stood at the kitchen window watching him, as he was aware, with her infinite scorn. Presently John's voice subsided to a mutter and Bessie knew he had seen Mrs. Truelove pass the hall window on her way downstairs. Bessie hastily turned to her soda biscuits. She pretended not to hear the light footsteps behind her, because she knew perfectly well that if John didn't say it Mrs. Truelove would.

"Well, Bessie! Up for the day?"

But Mrs. Truelove never waited for an answer to this pleasantry. She began humming "Ancient of Days" and puttering about the flour bin. She would not trust Bessie with the buckwheat cakes, though there was never a shadow on Bessie's soda biscuits.

"Sophie's helping the children to dress," she said. "George built a fire in their room. Sophie's going to town with Father on Saturday week to buy flannel for the children. They haven't any heavy nightgowns. Just imagine!"

Bessie, who slept in the greater part of her day clothing and then added a woolen wrapper for good measure, shivered sympathetically.

"Imagine no flannel nightgowns!" she exclaimed. "Their mother must be a queer one!" Then she stopped because you weren't supposed to talk outright about Lotta Truelove. That is—not to the family. Just to the neighbors, maybe, and then you had to take her part being almost a relation yourself—ten years in the family . . . Bessie tactfully switched the conversation. "Nice to have the young ones. I declare I do like children. Only none of 'em can come up to Mary Cecily's little Bobby."

Mrs. Truelove's cheek flushed faintly as it did whenever she thought of her oldest daughter, Mary Cecily. Her own child, really, just as Sophie was Stephen's child, a Truelove. Mary Cecily was quiet and sure and safe, a Mills through and through. She married and left them because a daughter should, and Cecily, the mother, rejoiced that one daughter at least would always do the comfortably suitable thing. But Sophie was like her father, something in her long silences sometimes terrified Cecily. She wanted to beat against the doors of that silence and cry, "Let me in, I say! I am your mother, Sophie—you can't—you daren't shut out your own people!"

"Mary Cecily is a good mother, Bessie," she said, then. "That's what makes a good child, always!"

Then the house seemed to shake on its foundations with the clatter of heavy boots in the hall. There was sneezing and loud trumpeting of noses.

"The men!" Bessie cried, as she did every morning, and flew to the oven to take out the biscuits. Tramp—tramp—tramp they sounded like a regiment.

"*Well,* Bessie! *Well,* Bessie! *Well,* Bessie! Up for the day, eh?"

And Bessie pouted and blushed and giggled. The Truelove men were a different matter from John—or Mrs. Truelove. Very different. George tweaked her ear.

"Now you stop!" giggled Bessie, flouncing over to the flour board. "Stop it, I say! You men!"

It was what Bessie said every morning.

Lois was dressed and Custer was dressed—except for the silly little necktie that went with his suit. But Vera lay serenely on the high feather bed, her thin arms folded over her head.

Sophie looked at her uncertainly. She had hoped to find in these children some trace of the Lotta Truelove whose pointed lovely face with its haunted eyes stared out of the album; she had, as a child, studied that picture breathlessly and thought, "This is the one I am like. Not like Cousin Caroline or Aunt Sadie or the others!" But Lotta's children bore none of their mother's magic, and Sophie was puzzled and disappointed. Only now and then something in Lois's profile, or in Vera's eyes.

Vera smiled at her wanly.

"Don't you think, Vera," Sophie hesitated, "you'd better get up? Lois is all ready and Custer—"

Vera did not move.

"I have consumption," she said, "I'm not supposed to get up when other people do. I shouldn't be surprised if it might kill me."

Lois shook her head gravely at Sophie.

"She always tells lies," she explained in a low voice. "Everything she says is a lie, Cousin Sophie, except when it hurts your feelings and then it's true."

She stood up on a chair before the bureau and brushed her fine mouse-colored hair before the little square mirror. She could part her own hair in the middle and tie her hair ribbons except when she didn't like them . . . The mirror was funny, it made you very fat and your head sort of squashed like in coffeepots.

"I like Vera best, Cousin Sophie," Custer confided. He looked like an infant caricature of his grandfather, Nathan Truelove, Sophie thought, standing there before the fireplace, his hands folded behind his skinny little back.

Lois climbed down from the chair.

"Custer," she informed Sophie, "is a very nasty child. He won't tell you when he wants to—" here she cupped her hands to her lips and whispered a euphemistic phrase—"and he really is a big boy, and Mother and I are ashamed of him."

Custer looked belligerent. Sophie smiled placatingly at him—these children really frightened her—and he relented.

"I can spell sailor," he said.

"Sophie! Hurry down with the children! Bessie has breakfast all ready!" Mrs. Truelove's voice came from the foot of the stairs. Then she thought her daughter might need help and she hurried up the steps.

"What? Isn't Vera up yet?"

Vera closed her eyes.

"She isn't asleep, Grandma," Lois said. "She's wide awake."

Mrs. Truelove went over to the great black walnut bed and looked down at Vera in bewilderment.

"Come, come, Vera! If you want to sleep—sleep, but nice little girls don't lie in bed when they're wide awake. That's slothfulness. Beds are to sleep in."

Vera opened one eye.

"How can I sleep with all you people talking?" she asked.

"That's being impudent, isn't it?" Lois hopefully inquired of her grandmother.

"Come, children. Bessie has griddle cakes and molasses waiting. We'll let Vera sleep."

Vera tumbled out of bed and scrambled madly into her clothes.

"Don't let them get there first," she implored Sophie, "There won't be any left."

But Lois was gleefully skipping down the stairs after her grandmother. Custer lingered behind, his head cocked meditatively.

"Cousin Sophie!" he called.

Sophie smiled at him.

"S-a-i-l-or" he said, "Sailor."

Grandmother Truelove slept late mornings. She didn't intend to and she blamed her daughter-in-law for it. It always seemed dark and early when she wakened and she was sure it must be, because her bones ached so wearily.

"Nobody's up yet," she would think triumphantly, "It can't be five yet. I'm eighty-six and I'm the first one awake in the house. I'm spryer than Cecily is at sixty."

But then she would hear Cecily's voice from the doorway.

"Well, Grandma, you did have a good sleep, didn't you? Slept right around the clock! Here it is half-past nine."

At this crushing news Grandma Truelove, hurt and irritated,

would shut her eyes and pretend not to hear. Now she heard loud yelping under her window and again her daughter-in-law's voice.

"Sophie, that child will have to be tied, that's all there is to it! That's the third time he's stepped on Tower's tail. I declare he does it on purpose. Hush, Custer! You'll wake Grandma."

"I am awake!" shrilly called Grandma from her mountain of comforters. As if she was a pampered, lazy old woman! As if she had to be treated like a baby! Hush, Custer, you'll wake Grandma indeed! . . . But that was just like Cecily Mills. A Mills she was—Mills all over. The whole lot of them were like that from Archie Mills, dead these forty years, down to Sadie Mills over on the Ridge. Cecily was just like the rest. She'd never make Stephen a good wife, never in all this world. . . . Thus did Grandma Truelove erase her son's forty years of married life.

Once settled in her low wicker chair by the living-room fire, the old lady did not stir all day except at mealtimes. To be sure on certain days, she would say thoughtfully, to show her daughter-in-law what an independent life she led, "I may get John to drive me down to see the Coles'."

"Now, Grandma!" Cecily would say indulgently, "Now, Grandma! At your age making that trip with roads the way they are! Why, it would shake you to pieces!"

"Yes," the old lady would pursue with dignity. "I may go over there today, if it's fine."

But of course she never did. Cecily would not have allowed it.

It annoyed her that Lotta's children should be unlike Lotta—not Trueloves at all—nor had any of them a particle of Lotta's haughty beauty. It bored her to have Lois and Custer stare at her intently for minutes at a stretch.

"Her face is all shirred," observed Lois. "Did it hurt?"

"No," said Grandma.

"Her fingers are all mixed up," added Custer. "I don't think she's any good."

Then he stole furtively to the window where Tiddledywinks, the younger collie, was napping, and yanked his tail with gratifying results.

"Where's Sophie?" demanded Grandma querulously. "I want my rags. I want to start a rug for Stephen's room. Little girl, go find Sophie."

This to Vera who came in from the parlor where she had been silently prying into all the cupboards and desk drawers.

"I'm not your slave," said Vera very softly.

"You're a bad little girl," exclaimed Grandma, aghast. "You do as I say or I'll give you a warming-up."

Vera was not sure what a warming-up was but the tone was menacing. She walked leisurely toward the kitchen as if she had been going to find Sophie anyway and old ladies need not think she was doing it for them. She found her cousin in the kitchen and delivered the message.

Sophie stood over the table, enveloped in a blue calico apron and whirled up the batter for a devil's food cake with her hands. White beautiful hands, they were, for her mother would not hear of her doing the sort of work other farm girls did—the Cole girls, for example.

Bessie stood at the other end of the table, sleeves pushed high over fat red arms, rolling out pie crust, but stealing glances now and then at Sophie's smooth tapering fingers—then looking back with woeful resignation to her own red swollen hands. It would be worth anything, she thought, to have Sophie Truelove's hands. . . . Sophie, knowing that her hands were flawless, dismissed them from her consideration, as she dismissed her white brilliant beauty because she knew it was there.

"Tell Grandma," she commanded Vera, "that I will be there as soon as the cake is in the oven."

Vera sat down.

"I guess she can wait," she said casually. "She's got all day. I want to make a cake."

Sophie made no reply nor did she look up. She was afraid of those slanting canny green eyes. It was strange to be afraid of a child . . . that fearfully knowing look that Grandmother Truelove had, too, so that one dared not look lest one reveal some truth one was hardly aware of; oneself . . . Oh, she was sadly disappointed in Aunt Lotta's children. She had hoped they would be touched with Lotta's strange world, that they would be warm lovely creatures she could hold in her arms and protect from the things she herself feared most. But these three self-sufficient little brutes . . . Sophie looked down at Vera's thin rapacious face—no-one would not dare to love her. Yet when their glances met there seemed a curious understanding between these two.

"I will show you how to make a cake," Sophie said, and picked up the measure. "You take the flour—this much—"

An elixir warm and buoyant stole into Grandmother Truelove when she looked at Sophie. Sometimes when she was half-dozing she was Sophie and that was a delicious experience. To be Sophie with swift leaping blood and sharp desires and awareness of beauty. Then again she was a numb old woman by the fire, and she was Sophie, then, too.

"She knows," Sophie on the footstool would think, the yarn unwinding between their four hands. "She might be on the stool and I might be she—an old Sophie in a wicker chair. Oh, I wish I were! I would know then. Things would have happened to me."

And the old Sophie and the young Sophie sat before the fire envying each other for knowing and for not knowing. And sixty-four years were strung on the thread between old Sophie's knowing eyes and young Sophie's wondering eyes. Sometimes a still determination would come in Sophie's face and the old woman would say to herself; "Now I am thinking—'I won't have any man if I can't have Nathan Truelove!'"—That was when Sophie was thinking, "That man on the post office steps . . . Other men don't matter . . . Why doesn't he hunt for me? Why doesn't he come? I'm twenty-two. If I wait for him to find me . . ."

"He will come," old Sophie would dream—only now she was young Sophie and not knowing—"He will want me."

She would smile then, a little wistful Sophie smile. But the girl saw only an old woman smiling to herself because she knew—because her fortune was finished—because for her there were no more wonders.

"When you go to town, Sophie," said Grandmother Truelove after a while, "I want you to bring me some hard candy. Sticks of it. Peppermint."

"I'll remember," said Sophie. She was thinking, "Even if it's storming I won't wear my greatcoat and knitted cap. I'll wear mother's sealskin cape and my feather toque. Because he might be coming over to Ashton that day. He might see me. But I shan't speak to him unless he comes up to me. He mustn't think I care about him."

Outside there was the sound of halloing in men's voices and the two collies barking.

"That's Stephen," said Grandmother Truelove happily. "Bring me my blue shawl, Sophie. Stephen likes blue."

"There's your father, Sophie," said Cecily, bustling in from the kitchen, a vegetable knife in her hand. "Hurry and get the table ready—the men will want to sit right down and eat."

"Is Bessie making corn pudding?" demanded Grandma. "I always used to have corn pudding for Stephen."

"There's stewed dried corn," Cecily answered quietly. "You see George never eats corn pudding."

The two mothers' eyes clashed for a moment fiercely and then the older woman blinked and turned away.

"Always *her* sons—*her* sons," she thought bitterly. "Never mine. Not even Stephen."

Cecily went back to the kitchen humming "Ancient of Days," a virtuous light in her eyes.

Dinner was very gay and noisy as it always was when the men brought letters and news from town. Bessie was radiant, giggling at everything the men said and proudly accepting their enormous appetites as a personal tribute.

"You stopped at Clem's then?" asked Grandmother Truelove. As if, Cecily thought, any farmer ever failed to stop at Clem Purvis's hardware store on a trip to town!

"Clem says Jerome Gardiner's been in town," said George, "while old Doc Gardiner was sick."

"Clem thinks Jerome'll be sent back to Washington again next year," added Stephen. "He's a clever boy, Jerome is. Smarter'n his dad."

"Boy!" Sophie exclaimed, "Why they say he's thirty at least!"

She was annoyed, then, that her father should laugh and pinch her cheek. Thirty was old. Mary Cecily was thirty-one and she belonged, you might say, to another generation. The nine years between them was as wide a bridge as that between herself and Grandmother Truelove. . . . And Jerome Gardiner had been a man as long as Sophie could remember. She had never seen him, for with schools and colleges and his law practice Jerome had been away over twelve years. But the Gardiners were a tradition and a part of the country as were the Trueloves and Hamiltons and the other New England families that had settled here a hundred years before. Their personal affairs were historical data in the neighborhood. Sophie, like everyone else, knew Jerome without ever having seen him, quite as well as she knew any of the neighbors she had grown up with.

"If he comes to Washington he can visit Mama," said Lois politely. She wanted more scalloped potatoes but Cousin George kept scooping and scooping—there wouldn't be any left. "I wish there was more potatoes, don't you, George?"

George was embarrassed.

"These Lotta's children?" asked John without enthusiasm. Three of the sickliest, nastiest little kids he ever saw. Not like Trueloves, except maybe the middle one whose eyes slanted in grotesque exaggeration of the family trait.

"Is Aunt Lotta still—well—" George was uncertain how far to go before Lotta's children, "still mixed up in astrology?"

Cecily nodded warningly toward the children. Lotta wasn't a person you could discuss before children, even her own.

"I'd like to see Lotta again," mused Stephen. "Nearly ten years since I saw her last. She ought to come back once in a while to her own folks. She was a beautiful girl twenty years ago, wasn't she, Mother?"

"The picture of Sophie, there, except for her yellow hair," agreed Grandmother Truelove. "Always a queer streak in her, though. You remember that, Stephen. Walked all day through the fields by herself. I never knew where she was."

"Good thing she married a city man," said Cecily. "She never would have done on a farm. Bessie, get Father more sausages."

Her toe was beating the floor nervously. She hated the tension that the mere mention of Lotta's name brought on the whole Truelove tribe. That moody look on Stephen's face—the way he looked . . . Oh, she could tell, when he was thinking of Lotta or of that other woman thirty years ago . . . She hated that look. She hated Lotta for bringing it. And she hated the way they always compared the young Lotta to Sophie. Her tall beautiful Sophie.

Look at her, now. Sitting there with a little excited flush on her face, not eating a thing, her eyes shining as if she *wanted* to do the things Aunt Lotta had done! . . . Cecily quickly shut it out of her mind.

"Exact picture of Sophie there, eh, Stephen?" the old woman repeated.

Sophie could not eat. There was a spell in Aunt Lotta's very name. Would she too, have those strange things happen to her that happened to Aunt Lotta? Things that caught her up and carried her away from Trueloves and fields and farms? Would people shake their heads when they talked of her, as they did over Aunt Lotta? Or what would happen to her? What would happen? She was twenty-two. Time for the things to happen that were meant to happen. Things special to her. She would not be content with other women's joys—this farmer proposing, that one begging to call. It was time for the strange things that were meant for Sophie Truelove alone. Time—then Sophie saw Grandma Truelove sitting at the foot of the table, smug, complacent, devoid of all wonder and a fury of envy swept her. *She* knew. Oh, *she* didn't have to wonder!

"The Hamiltons were in town last week," offered George. Seems they're doing some trading in Ashton Center, Clem says, since the Middletown store burned. Lynn's back now."

"Is Lynn back?" John asked. "He must be a full-grown man, now."

"I haven't seen Dora Hamilton in six years," said Cecily. "It was at the Fair. We used to be such friends when we were girls, too."

"I want some mince pie," said Custer, who had silently gorged himself for several minutes.

"He can't have it," said Lois. "It's bad for him. And Vera can't either because she didn't eat any dinner."

"Will you look at that?" exclaimed Grandma, pointing to Vera's plate, which was laden with piccalilli and nothing else.

"That's all she's eaten. Three big plates of piccalilli. Cecily, that child will be sick."

"No, she won't," Sophie said absently. The Hamiltons, then—Lynn Hamilton was back, George had said. In a flash she knew that the stranger on the post office steps must have been he. Ah, now she remembered . . . that church picnic years ago. Someone had lifted her into a swing. She had sat there clinging to the ropes, her starched ruffles standing out in yellow petals all about her, her small slippered feet stiffly horizontal. Her father had given the swing a push and then left her swaying. Swings frightened her, but only a boy with blue eyes under the tree would know that.

"There's nothing to be scared about," he had said, "I'll catch you if you fall." And so reassured Sophie swung higher and higher and presently she forgot her fear and the boy pushing her and knew only the ecstasy of flying. Higher—higher—the boy said his name was Lynn Hamilton from Middletown on the other side of the Ridge and she had never seen him since. But she remembered now his blue eyes. Different from men's eyes staring at her in church, eyes of men who might do for other women. . . . She was eager for George to tell more about him but she dared not ask bold questions.

John helped her.

"How was Lynn?" he asked. Dear John!

"Lynn? Why, you know his dad sent him to Lorain a year or so back," obliged George—dear George!—"He was pretty restless and the old man didn't think he'd ever be satisfied to marry and settle down on the farm. But Lynn couldn't stand the city, Clem said. Said he wanted to be where he knew folks. So he's back now and Clem says he's settled down there on the farm and you couldn't hire him to leave. That's farming blood."

"He'll get the three hundred acres up by the woods when his uncle dies," said Stephen.

Sophie tore up a biscuit and said never a word. If he went to the Center to trade then she would see him next Saturday when she went in with John and Father. He would remember the swing, surely. He would speak and perhaps . . . She would wear her blue broadcloth and the sealskin cape—it was worn but it was rich-looking—and the little brown hat with drooping feathers.

"Mother, you haven't eaten a thing," Stephen rebuked his mother.

"She never eats anything." Cecily answered. "Never anything but biscuits and syrup."

"Cecily, I do eat other things," said Grandmother Truelove haughtily. "It just happens that today I—I—"

She forgot what she started to say. That happened at noon always when she was so drowsy. But she did remember that Cecily had said something to annoy her and that the dignified thing to do would be to proudly leave the table. So she asked Sophie to help her to her chair by the fire, ignoring Cecily's protestations.

"Well, young man," said John, aware that Custer's eyes had not left his face since he sat down. "Well! So your name's Custer, eh?"

"What of it?" Custer defied him.

Lois swallowed an amazing portion of pie at a gulp.

"You'll have to excuse Custer, John," she said. "He's just awful. If you want to act polite to us, maybe you'd better talk to me."

"Lois is a little lady," said Cecily approvingly.

Sophie poured a second round of coffee and Bessie carried the cups around. Sophie did not speak lest the men should start on another subject. She must hear more about Lynn Hamilton.

"Yes sir, Jerome Gardiner's a mighty smart fellow," said John, tilting his chair back. "He'll be a big man some day. You wait."

Stupid John! Sophie poured another cup for him.

"Some smart-looking horses he had sent out," chuckled George.

(Stupid George! Who cared about Jerome Gardiner's horses?) "Clem said he had some sure winners there. Clem said if Jerome ever wanted to give up politics he had a neat fortune right in his stable. Three blue ribbons he took home from the State Fair last year."

"Old Doc told Clem that Jerome never came home to see him anymore," said John. Stupid, stupid John! Who cared whether Jerome Gardiner ever came home? Who cared about his old horses? Not Sophie Truelove, that was certain. She clenched her hand tightly under the table.

"Said he just came to see his horses. Clem says he pays Fred Tompkins twenty dollars a month and keep just to look after those horses."

"I should think if he was as smart a man as you say," Sophie could endure it no longer, "he would find something better to do with his spare time than play with racing horses! A lawyer wasting his time that way! I don't think he's so smart."

Stephen roared and pinched her cheek again, and Sophie flushed.

"Don't you fool yourself, Sophie," he said seriously. "He knows more than horses and law. He's been brought up on his dad's books and old Doc Gardiner has one of the finest libraries in the country. Doc says the boy's got a better one himself in Washington. But don't you fool yourself. Jerome Gardiner's a smart man."

Sophie pretended not to hear. Oh, why were men so stupid? As if anyone there cared about the Gardiners! Spending a whole dinner hour talking about a man they never saw except at the State Fair or when he came home once or twice a year to see his father!

"Clem says he's a little weak with women," said George.

"The Gardiner men are always weak with women," pronounced Grandma Truelove from her corner by the fireplace.

"Well, Mother, I guess every family has its cracked streak," said Stephen. "Sometimes it crops out in the men and sometimes in the women."

"How can you say such things, Stephen?" Cecily scolded. She remembered Lotta and was silent.

George pushed back his chair and got to his feet.

"Dad, how about them stalls?" he said. "John says you figure on hauling the logs from Coles' place over to the sawmill first thing tomorrow morning."

It was the signal for the men to get up. They went out to the kitchen and sat around, pulling on their high boots and sweaters. Cecily and Bessie began clearing up the table with a great rattling of dishes and knives and forks. Sophie lingered at the table, stirring her coffee cup. She felt helpless—beaten. She wanted to ask if Lynn Hamilton had blue eyes—it must be him she had seen that day—but you couldn't ask. . . .

Custer sat beside her, rapidly and unobtrusively spooning out sugar from the sugar bowl. Sophie looked at him and he put the spoon down quickly and rubbed his sleeve across his sugary face.

"I don't like mince pie, anyway," he said somberly. "Nor Grandma, neither."

Snow had fallen for two nights and a day. It lay drifted against the farmhouse, above the windowsills and high against the stables. Fences were buried and the roads hidden. Below the orchard the shallow creek was frozen in a pattern of ferns and dead leaves. Over it leaned bushes tangled with snow, their brittle fingers caught in each other's hair. The earth was a blare of white for acres and acres.

From the kitchen door to the Truelove stable there were deep footprints, a scattering of snow where the cutter had been dragged out, and deep narrow ruts from the stable out to the main road, for Sophie and her father and John had driven to town. No sooner had the Truelove cutter vanished over the hill than another sleigh appeared in the lane and drew up close to the barn. It was the Anderson girls come to call, and as Cecily said, they could not have timed their call more opportunely, for Sophie usually ignored them and Stephen laughed at them. With only Cecily and Grandma present, however, they were bound to have more satisfaction for their greedy curiosity.

They had stopped on their way to the Ridge, they said, to see if Cecily wanted anything from Hartley's Big Store. But Cecily knew they only wanted to find out about Lotta and what the arrival of her three children meant. One of the Trueloves in trouble, it must be that—Lotta again, they had probably rejoiced.

People still called them the "Anderson girls" just as they had when the two wore crinoline and knitted hopefully for young men at war who would later marry other girls. They drove up in their antique cutter and delicately waved mittened hands toward the house. George helped to excavate them from their lap robes while they twittered the reason for their call.

"I don't think Mother will want anything from Hartley's." George drawled. "We do most of our trading at the Center now. Sophie and Dad just drove over there today and I reckon they'll get what they want there."

"At least we can stop for a little chat," Lucy Anderson said in her thin china voice. "And we can see Lotta's babies."

George smiled a little grimly as the two old ladies swayed along the path John had shoveled to the house.

Cecily saw them coming from the kitchen window and her face grew curiously white. It was strange that even now she could not see these two women without blanching. At sight of them a long-dead monster reared its ghastly head before Cecily Truelove, she could see it gleaming behind their pale old eyes, could hear its voice behind their words. . . . But this was foolish. They would never speak of that secret thing anymore than she herself would. They had come to pry into Lotta's affairs this time. That was bad enough, but Lotta's adventures were easier spoken of than that other fearful thing. . . .

Cecily braced herself and held out her hands.

"Well, Lucy! Well, Sara!"

She led them into the living room where Grandma sat teaching the three children to embroider doilies. Perversely enough Grandma gave the two sisters an uncommonly warm welcome, though she knew as well as Cecily that they had come to ask about Lotta.

"Fancy Lotta having three little ones!" said Lucy, fixing her protuberant bright eyes on Custer. "And she tells fortunes, they say."

Grandma's eyes narrowed.

"Show Miss Anderson how nicely you can embroider," she urged Custer.

"What fortunes?" demanded Custer, staring insolently at the callers. Cecily sat down on the edge of a dining chair and kept silent.

"Let's see, their father's name was Palmer, wasn't it?" Sara asked very sweetly. "We were speaking of it at the Cole's last night—Matt Cole ran off with the schoolteacher, you heard, I suppose—not Fred at all as we had thought—and Tess said she thought Lotta had married a Winton."

Cecily smiled at Grandmother Truelove. Lotta was a Truelove, not of her blood, thank God. Let the old woman defend her, then, before the community. Palmer was the man Lotta had eloped with, let her explain, from this very farm. Winton was the man she left Palmer for. Horatio Winton, the Southern senator who had to give up his career because of the divorce scandal. And let her tell, too, of the Hindu mystic Lotta had been seen with in New York, the one people said she might actually marry after she separated from Winton. But it wasn't because she was a bad woman that Cecily hated her, it was because of her wicked black arts. Lotta was a witch, Cecily thought. She, Cecily, a mature woman, had been afraid of her twenty years before when Lotta was barely twenty-five, with her masses of ash-gold hair and strange slanting eyes.

"They're all Wintons," said Grandma Truelove comfortably. "Lotta had no children by her first husband. Here, Custer, let Grandma show you how to hold the needle."

"I will not," said Custer, and crawled under the table.

"Look, Grandma," said Lois. "He blew his nose on his doily."

"Lois is working her doily in red and green," explained Grandma, "and Vera is working hers in pink and blue. I think they are doing very well, don't you, Sara?"

"Very nice, indeed," said Sara primly. "Very nice, I'm sure. Is their mother well?"

"She has consumption," said Vera proudly. "And so have I."

"Oh, what a lie, Vera Winton!" gasped Lois. "Oh, what a whopper! Mama's perfectly well and so are you and you know it!"

"That's good," exclaimed Lucy, giving Sara a long look that said, "She has consumption, you see. You heard what the child said. Children never lie."

And Sara gave Lucy a look that said, "Of course she has consumption. Anyone who has two husbands *should* have consumption."

"So Stephen went to town, eh?" asked Sara. Cecily did not answer for an instant. Now, they had dropped Lotta and were coming to the other. Oh, no matter what they might say, she knew it was in their minds whenever they spoke Stephen's name. Then she heard herself speaking quite naturally.

"Yes, he will be sorry to have missed you."

But the Anderson girls were blurred shadows before her eyes and the spacious room was suddenly that red and gilt hotel room in Columbus. Twenty years ago . . . It was all because of Lotta, Cecily always felt, for she had written Stephen to visit Kate Maxwell when he got to the Capitol. Lotta had known what would happen. A witch, she was, whose evil spell neither absence nor years could banish. Kate Maxwell . . . Cecily saw her now clearly through the shade that Lucy Anderson had suddenly become. Kate, big and blonde and laughing, in that tight black velvet dress, sitting on the arm of Stephen's chair—a young, fair Stephen, too, even though he was the head of a family. And there she, the wife, sat smiling to see them laughing at each other, pretending that she saw no harm in that mock lovemaking, that she thought it was a huge joke, too. Smiling, smiling, seated in the hotel room that night when he didn't come back at all, when he said he was seeing certain officials about the plow invention he had made—smiling to see him kiss Kate good-bye, both of them with that queer look in their eyes—always smiling stiffly when she burned with a steel-bright hate, when the smile tortured her so that she could have shrieked, shrieked with her two thin arms beating the air, "I know, you Two. I know! I'm little and quiet and so you two great laughing beasts make love over my head, yes, over my body! I smile—and you think you've fooled me— but I know, and I could kill you and your bigness and your laughing!"

Then back on the farm again with Stephen quiet and moody, writing to Lotta—as if there were things he could say to her that he could not say to his own wife! And finally the day the Anderson girls came to call, "My dear, we feel we should tell you. . . . We were in Columbus at a certain hotel . . . and Stephen . . ." She had not let them go on. "Please don't bother," she had said, and wondered how her voice came above a gasp. "I know all about it. I was there. It's quite easily explained, but I don't feel that I want to explain to you. Good-bye Sara, good-bye, Lucy." They had said no more, though there was always faint mockery in their eyes when they looked at her.

Then the letter that came many years later begging Stephen to come to her. She was dying, Kate wrote, and he was the only man she had ever loved.

"I ask so little, darling Stephen. Only to have you touch my hand, or if that is too much, only to hear your dear laugh. In another three months I shall be dead."

Cecily tore up the letters and Stephen never knew of them. There were three or four. And when Cecily tore them, it was not paper but a big, blonde laughing woman in a tight velvet dress she was tearing. As for Stephen, he knew of Kate a year later through the Columbus cousins. Cecily had watched his face when he asked about her.

"Kate Maxwell? She died eight months ago in San Francisco. Lungs, I believe," they had said, and Cecily had looked away from the gray revelation in Stephen's face.

Cecily saw the Anderson girls again, old now, with avid spinsters' eyes and sagging fish mouths. Under her breath she chanted "Ancient of Days, who sitteth throned in glory," steadily, absorbingly until the horrible ghost had lain down. Kate Maxwell was dead. She, Cecily, had conquered. With her two quiet hands she had torn her rival to bits, and now she was at peace. Only when she saw those Anderson women and remembered what they were remembering . . . Cecily shivered suddenly. Grandmother Truelove was looking at her.

"Sara asked you if she could bring the new schoolteacher to call some evening," Grandma said petulantly. "She's not going to stay at the Hamilton's much longer because it's too far to school. She's going to move over to the Anderson's place the first of the month, they say. Why can't you talk, Cecily?"

"Of course we'd like to meet her," Cecily said quickly.

"She's a dear little thing," said Lucy. "From the south."

"Steubenville," added Sara. "She's a second cousin of Dora Hamilton but not a bit like her."

"She'll be such company for us," said Lucy.

"These children will have to go over to the schoolhouse next term," said Grandma Truelove, "Stephen said so. Would you like to meet your teacher, Lois?"

"Not for a while, Grandma," said Lois politely. "I don't think Mother would want me to."

Sara and Lucy exchanged a cautious look again.

"Strange that Lotta doesn't miss her little ones," ventured Lucy. "Or perhaps she doesn't trust her own influence."

"She'll be coming soon," Grandma said calmly. "She's just sent them on ahead."

Cecily caught her breath at this nice bit of fancy.

"Do bring the schoolteacher to see us," she broke in hastily. "What is she like? I suppose she'll marry right off, just like the last one."

"Probably," and then Lucy innuendoed, "Sophie isn't engaged yet, is she?"

"Truelove women aren't so easy suited," retorted Cecily blandly. "Sophie's waiting until she finds a man good enough for her. There aren't many, you know, good enough for a girl like Sophie."

Lucy Anderson delicately adjusted the yellowing sealskin coat about her throat. Her sister followed her example.

"Sara and I always said it was such a pity Sophie couldn't have had Jerome Gardiner," said Lucy gently. "Such a fine man, what we hear of him."

"He married a Washington woman," said Sara, and added regretfully. "It's so hard to find out anything about her. Doctor Gardiner is so reserved. I'm afraid there must be something odd about it."

"He never even saw Sophie," said Grandma Truelove.

"Too bad," said Lucy sweetly. "It would have been so nice to have her married and off your minds."

"Such a pretty girl, Sophie is," breathed Sara. "What are the young men thinking of, I wonder?"

"Of course," said Lucy with a little laugh. "Young men nowadays don't like a proud girl and they do say that Sophie is that."

"Or cold," said Sara. "No matter how pretty a girl is, if she's too cold . . ." Sara coughed and finished her sentence by shaking her head smilingly.

When they got up to go neither Cecily nor old Mrs. Truelove urged them to stay. They pecked at Grandma's cheek in farewell and went back to their sleigh. Cecily stood at the window waving to them, smiling brightly and humming her hymn insistently to keep from thinking of the thing they recalled to her. Grandma resumed her embroidery lessons.

"Naughty boy, Custer," she scolded. "You haven't done a bit. Nor you, Lois. Just listening to the grown-ups talk. But just see what Vera has done. That's Grandma's little girl."

Vera triumphantly displayed her work, a round smudgy doily worked in a bumpy leprous design of pink, blue, red, and green silk.

"She took all my red and green thread!" Lois cried indignantly. "She stole all the thread. She was just to have pink and blue."

"Hush, Grandma's nervous!" rebuked the old lady. "You are a very naughty little girl not to embroider the way Grandma showed you."

"But how could I?" wailed Lois. "She took all my thread."

But Grandma nodded her head and dozed off. Vera slid virtuously away, her handiwork in her pocket, leaving Lois sobbing loudly and Custer under the table snapping his jaws the way Tiddleydwinks did.

"Gr-r—r—r-r-wow," he said presently.

Sophie had only to go to town on a market day to know that she was beautiful. She sat between her father and John in the sleigh, her fur coat drawn up over her chin, her legs snug under the great bearskin lap robe and the wind whipping her ivory face to scarlet. Once on the main road to Ashton Center all the vehicles slowed in passing and men leaned out to stare at her. Sometimes the thin wintry air would carry their nasal comments back to her.

"No, Sir, Bill—can't think who it would be. Must be the Truelove girl. She's the beauty in these parts, you know. Old Stephen's girl."

Then Sophie's eyes would flash a little and John, red and puckered from the cold, would chuckle and her father would smile and say, "Eh, Sophie? Did you hear that?"

"Men are so silly," she would answer. "Why Father, they knew I could hear. How dared they?"

And Stephen would wink at John and pinch her cheek.

Presently they came into town, a scattering of jaunty little houses and half a dozen stores, their roofs all capped with snow. All along the street bobsleds and sleighs were hitched, and the snow was strewn with straw from the sleds. The Truelove sleigh drew up in front of Clem Purvis's hardware store. Behind Clem's windows could be seen several farmers in corduroys, fur caps, and great hip boots, for Clem's was the farmers' meeting place just as the dingy little poolroom over the post office was the town men's rendezvous. In the back of Clem's store around the big base burner classic—discussions were held concerning Bryan, horse-less carriages, bicycle races, and the problems of the day. The smell of new nails and machine oil stimulated senses used to less sophisticated odors, and stirred reluctant tongues to eloquence.

While the men gathered in Clem's, the women would be gossiping and shopping in the musty little dry goods store across the street. It was here that John and Stephen left Sophie while they went into Clem's. But Sophie did not go in the store immediately. She stood for an instant before the window display and sent a cautious look down the road to see if the Hamilton team was anywhere in sight. It was not. . . . There were the boys shouting to her from their huge sled, and the Coles—Mrs. Cole and the twins bundled up in horse blankets, and the Greers—the half-wit brother grinning foolishly at her from the driver's seat—but no sight of Hamiltons in town.

Tears of vexation came to Sophie's eyes.

"Nothing ever happens the way it should," she thought. "He should be there in front of Clem's and he should look at me the way he did that other time—and then. . . ."

And then she was at the door of the dry goods store and Lynn Hamilton was coming out, holding the door open for her, looking down at her with curious intensity.

The sight of him startled Sophie into a deep blush. She lowered her head quickly and went into the store. Out of the corner of her eye she saw him standing out in front, his wide felt hat slanting down over his eyes, his bare hands thrust into the pockets of his corduroys. He was a lithe handsome figure with a lazy swagger that seemed to fascinate the town girls. They paraded up and down the little street as they always did on market day, giggling whenever they passed him. Now and then a man on a sleek black horse galloped up the street and back and the girls forgot Lynn to stare after the rider.

"That's Mr. Gardiner on his prize filly," said Mrs. Moore, behind the counter.

"Yes?" commented Sophie. "I want a bolt of blue flannel."

How different Lynn was from other farm men! She remembered that feeling she had had that as a boy he was as set apart from other boys as she was from other girls. That long ago day neither had mingled with the children's groups. . . . Now he did not even turn around to look at Sophie but stood near the curb with two other men admiring the black horse that had paused impatiently at its rider's command. Men admired horses more than they did women, no use denying it. . . . Sophie's head tossed. She would not admit to herself that she had any interest in the young man outside, since he would not turn. There were amenities to be exchanged with Mrs. Moore and other women who came into the store to finger goods and buy their calicoes or percales. Sophie could hear them whispering behind her.

"She knows she's a Truelove all right. Pretty, yes, if you like that black and white kind. No color in her cheeks. Quiet, too. Thinks she's too good for the young men around here. . . Past twenty . . . better look out she'll be an old maid yet. These proud ones are the ones that get left. . . ."

Sophie's head in the little feathered toque went a trifle higher. She didn't care. These were the women who had married the only men who asked them, as their rosy buxom daughters would do after them. But she was Sophie. She would take nothing unless it be of her own fanciful choosing. Be an old maid, then! Be like the Anderson girls—and yet—that steady glance from Lynn Hamilton's eyes had meant more than admiration. There was purpose in it. . . . Ah, no, she would not be like the Anderson girls. Even if he did ignore her, standing out there—but did he? Sophie could not resist turning around. Across the street the black horse was standing in the midst of a group of men from Clem's store. Its owner, a dark man in high riding boots, his soft hat thrust under his arm, smilingly received the compliments of the other men. Nearby was a smaller group, and here Sophie saw Lynn Hamilton with Ferd Lewis and Hart Purvis encircling a thin young woman in badly-fitting blue broadcloth with a worn moleskin cape-collar and hat. She had a pale, pinched blue little face, watery blue eyes that half closed to send oblique glances upward at each man as he spoke. And her upper teeth kept catching nervously at her underlip and gnawing it so that tiny drops of blood stood on the dry chafed lip. Sophie could hear her thin little laugh, almost hear her teeth chattering with cold when she made an arch answer to one of Hart Purvis's sallies.

Who was she? Why was Lynn Hamilton smiling down at her? . . . But he looked up when Sophie came out.

"Upon my soul, Sophie Truelove!" exclaimed Hart, stretching a great hand toward her. "Here's a little lady that wants to make friends out your way. Little Anna Stacey. Come up to take the Ridge school. Staying out at Lynn's folks. Meet Miss Truelove, Anna. Those two ought to be friends, eh, Lynn?"

Sophie and the new schoolteacher exchanged an edged smile. The latter drew from her woolen muff a small clammy hand for Sophie to shake.

"I don't like her," Sophie thought. Then she was aware of Lynn Hamilton's eyes fixed on her, appraising, admiring, with a quiet assurance in them that frightened her a little.

"I've been wanting to meet you for a long time, Miss Sophie," he drawled. "Ever since . . .

"Ever since . . . ?" challenged Sophie.

"Ever since," he said and smiled down at her. "Are you still afraid of swings?"

"No," answered Sophie, "I learned to like them very much."

Sophie looked away from him with an effort because she knew the pale little schoolteacher was watching them, as if; Sophie thought, Lynn Hamilton were her fiancé. But now Sophie felt kind toward her. She could afford to be kind to her from now on, she thought.

"That's a beautiful beast over there, isn't she?" Ferd said, following the direction of Sophie's eyes to the group in front of Clem's. "Won three blue ribbons last year, you know. Young

Gardiner knows a thoroughbred—if you don't believe me, just notice how he keeps looking your way."

He laughed and Sophie hastily looked back at Lynn.

"Don't forget to tell your folks, Sophie," Hart was saying.

"But what is it?" Sophie appealed to Lynn. "I didn't hear. . . ."

He was insolently handsome, she thought, with his soft hat pulled down that way and his short, sheep-lined corduroy jacket instead of the greatcoats other farmers wore. Strength was in his shoulders, though he was little above average height.

"It's a party at our place for folks to meet Anne here," Lynn explained. "You're to tell your folks to come. But you needn't plan to go home with them."

"Why?" asked Sophie in a voice as level as his own.

He paused to stuff some tobacco leisurely into his pipe.

"Because I'm going to drive you home in my cutter," he said calmly.

Sophie colored and looked across the way. The dark man was on his horse again, a broad, erect figure, his hat in his hand. The thoroughbred reared and whirled about; its rider looked at Sophie. As they galloped past Sophie looked after them absently.

"You will come?" Lynn urged her.

"Of course," said Sophie. "What a beautiful horse!"

The little teacher laughed a thin trickling laugh and dabbed her handkerchief at the bit of blood on her gnawed lip.

Everyone was going to the Hamilton party except Cecily and Grandma and the children. Sophie helped Bessie to dress because Bessie's dress had all sorts of mysterious fastenings down the back that Bessie's clumsy fingers could not reach. Bessie wanted to be laced, too, a crime in which Mrs. Truelove would never aid her.

Bessie had removed her kitchen dress when Sophie came into her room, and was bending over the washbowl, gingerly washing her neck. Her black knitted petticoat was pinned up over her corset, and her gray woolen underwear rolled down at the neck to the approximate line on her bosom where the green dress would come. Her sandy hair was twisted into a loose topknot.

"I'm so excited," she giggled to Sophie. "Aren't you?"

Sophie sat down on the bed and drew her soft wrapper about her with a little shiver. She was excited, surely she was excited, and yet never had she felt more tranquil, more strangely peaceful.

"It's because I'm not waiting for something to happen any more," she thought. "It is happening."

When Bessie was properly fastened she would go to her own room and put on a pale blue challis that Mary Cecily had made for her last spring—her pearl eardrops—her hair high.

Bessie dropped her petticoat to the floor, kicked off her shoes. She pulled off her corset and the gray underwear. She reached for a large tin and obscured herself in a cloud of heavily scented powder. Sophie opened a drawer of the highboy and handed her a suit of underwear. Bessie turned her back and nervously tried to step into the legs. The back view of Bessie naked with her head bent forward was a double heart shape. Her great shoulders lifted, the slope to the waist, and then the enormous buttocks tapering down to the knees. Sophie looked away. Women naked were shameful sights. . . . Sophie picked up a scrap of paper that had fallen to the floor. A list of names was written on it.

"What is this, Bessie?" she asked.

Bessie turned.

"Men who have kissed me," she answered with pride. "I keep a list. Just for fun."

Sophie gasped. She quickly turned the paper over lest she see names written there that she might know. But there were more names on the other side.

"And this . . .

"What? Oh, that's another list. . . ." Bessie said, reddening a little. She giggled.

Sophie shrank into her wrapper and dropped the paper with haste. She was ashamed of having touched the paper, indeed of being in the same room with this Bessie she had not known. She rose abruptly, knowing that her face revealed her distaste.

"Do hurry, Bessie," she said, making an effort to be natural, "or I can't take time to draw your laces."

"Oh, please, Sophie," Bessie cried, frantically struggling with the corset, "I have to be laced. That green dress shows off my figure so well."

Sophie was nauseated now. She did not want to look at Bessie. Bessie, plump, effulgent, with her wide hips, swollen breasts, thick pink arms and thighs, was not a woman but a fat lazy sow for breeding and for boars' delight. Sophie was conscious of a fierce ascetic revulsion at the thought of what pleasure Bessie's curves promised.

"Carnal—vile!" she shuddered. . . . Yet whenever she thought of those vague pleasures for herself; for Sophie Truelove, she did not shudder. Rather she was consumed with a fierce white exultation. It was not carnal nor was the thought a physical desire when it was Sophie. Then it was the simple need of her spirit.

A few minutes later she was in her own room drawing the blue challis gratefully over her own slim delicious body, and there was a warmth in her breast at the thought of seeing Lynn Hamilton.

The Hamilton fields spread southward over two hundred acres to the cobblestone wall that was the boundary between Middletown and Ashton Ridge. The house itself was built in a variety of balconies and cupolas, a wandering piazza edged it, stopping politely on the south side to allow a conservatory to bulge out. It was considered by both Middletown and Ashton people to be a very handsome house and was pointed out, with its cupola-studded barn and granaries as one of the showplaces of the upper county.

Lynn's own mother was long dead and the second Mrs. Hamilton was a fat, company-loving soul who kept up her spirits by entertaining for seasons at a stretch distant relatives of either Tom's or her own. It broke her heart that Anna Stacey could not stay with them all spring, but they were eleven miles from the Ridge schoolhouse where Anna was to teach, and Anna was obliged to take quarters with the Anderson girls who lived just below the Ridge.

For the party Mrs. Hamilton had called in the Cole girls and her own Jenny's cousins to help decorate the attic ballroom and make cakes and cookies and doughnuts. There were twelve roast chickens and two iron kettles of potato salad sitting on the kitchen table and plates stacked high on the sideboard. Half a dozen coffeepots were bubbling on the stove. In the dining room, gloomily impressive with its antlered deer's head, moose head and lithograph of a huge salmon, all the lamps were lighted. Six tall candles burned on the snowy dining table and here reigned a great cut-glass bowl of cherry bounce, flanked by mounds of doughnuts and lavishly-iced chocolate cakes.

Mrs. Hamilton was red and enormous in a plum-colored taffeta, appallingly snug so that the boning of the bodice was outlined in the back and her mountainous bosom pushed way up above the armpits. She panted from kitchen to attic and then to the spare bedroom where the ladies would uncloak. From time to time she would stand outside Anna Stacey's room and say, "Ann! It's seven o'clock. Folks will be here any minute now."

"Yes, Dora, I'm coming," Anna would say and would pinch her cheeks some more to make them pink, and cock her head before the mirror this way and that to see which pose was more becoming. She wanted Lynn to admire her this last night she was spending at his house. He had said he would come to see her after she settled at the Andersons', and, though he had not yet smiled at her the way he had at the Truelove girl, still she could win him. She could not storm her way to triumph, perhaps the way handsome women did. No, but there were ways of winning men. Sometimes one did not realize one's own charm. . . . He had been kind to her ever since she had come to his house and once—only yesterday—he had told her that blue was becoming to her.

Long before half-past seven the guests were arriving. Some had started immediately after five o'clock supper because for those nearer the Center it was a good three hour drive. From the windows Mrs. Hamilton watched for the sleds—lanterns swinging from the front seat—to wind around the driveway. Then she would hear Tom's voice, "Hi, Fred, Hi, Molly!" and she would rush again to the stairs. "Anna! Anna! The Greers are here . . . and I think the Jepsons. . ." But Anna did not come down until a quarter of eight. Then she rubbed a chamois over her nose, pulled the gray satin over her thin shoulder blades and made sure that the starched ruffles in her bosom were suitably adjusted. She had a little twisted smile when she came down the staircase. Tonight was her night.

"Good evening, Lynn," she said softly when she got to the foot of the stairs.

Lynn turned sharply. He had been peering into the dining room and then the parlor where Elizabeth Jepson was playing the organ. (She was the Minister's wife and was expected to be musical.) He was very handsome and didn't care whether he was or not. Nor had he troubled to wear Sunday clothes but wore a soft-collared tan shirt with his corduroys and high-laced boots.

Ann stood beside him a moment with a demure upward glance. Lynn mumbled some remark, his eyes roving toward the window where new arrivals could be seen in the lantern glow.

"Hurry, Anna, the Trueloves—oh, I see you're down." It was Mrs. Hamilton again. She beamed at Lynn. She really was devoted to her stepson, having had no children of her own. "The Trueloves have just come."

Lynn's face became oddly constrained.

"Do you think gray is too old for me?" the little schoolteacher was asking coyly.

"Er-no," Lynn said confusedly. They were coming through the side door, the Truelove men, the fat giggling hired girl, and the arrogantly beautiful daughter. Sophie's sealskin cape was thrown back and a rose-colored lace muffler fluttered down with glimpses of pale blue underneath. She saw Lynn, nodded gravely to him and then followed Mrs. Hamilton to the spare bedroom.

Lynn straightened his shoulders and swung into the parlor. He left Anna at the foot of the steps staring after him, her fingernails tearing into her bloodless palms.

Stephen Truelove and Doc Gardiner stood at one end of the ballroom and watched the young people dancing. Near them sat the musicians, Jerry Coles at the piccolo, little Johnny Maxwell at the snare drum, and Martin Haynes, the Ashton Ridge barber, at the fiddle. The eaves sloped over them and the raw beams were covered with pine branches.

"Your girl is a beauty, Stephen," said the old doctor, his eyes on Sophie. "Will you let her marry any of the boys hereabouts?"

"Sophie'll take who she wants," replied Stephen imperturbably. "Any man that's good enough for Sophie is good enough for me. Sophie won't tolerate anything second-rate."

The doctor twisted the ends of his white beard.

"Looks like Lotta, you know, Stephen," he mused. "I saw Lotta last time I visited Jerome in Washington. She's a fine-looking woman, Stephen, that sister of yours. Don't look much over thirty in spite of all she's gone through."

"Lotta's forty," said Stephen. "Twenty-two years between us, Doctor. She was the youngest, you know. Might almost have been my daughter. . . . Did she seem happy?"

He did not like to ask strangers about his own sister—strangers discussed that sister enough as it was. But Lotta seldom wrote the truth about herself, and anyway Doctor Gardiner was not a stranger. He had been more than half in love with Lotta long ago. . . .

The doctor's foot was unconsciously beating time to the music.

"No, I don't think Lotta's happy," he said slowly. "She lives well—in luxury. But when we talked that old restlessness was there. Lotta'll never be satisfied. You know, Stephen, some women have something in them that will never let them be happy. Lotta will always be like that. Men—stars—crystal gazing—black magic—theosophy—."

"She's not that bad, Jay!" protested Stephen.

The doctor shrugged his shoulders.

"Perhaps not yet. In another five years—yes. Then more Hindu cults—or possibly another husband.

Stephen frowned.

"You're making Lotta out much more foolish than she is, Jay," he rebuked.

The older man made a gesture of apology.

"Don't misunderstand," he said, "Lotta's no worse and no different from dozens of women—all these women who have emotions they don't know what to do with. It comes out in some queer streak. . . . They're never happy. Even your Sophie— smiling over there—I wonder if even she is happy."

Stephen's eyes grew tender as they dwelt on his daughter. What could she know of misery, of heavy sorrow? He, Stephen, knew. Misery was a rooted weed in his bosom. For him there would never be peace. He would go on forever wondering about a woman who had forgotten him long, long ago, a woman who had given him flame and stars—but she had died forgetting him. He would never have left Cecily for her—Kate had understood that—but they two had sworn never to forget. He had written— but no letter had ever come for him, no sign that those hours had meant to her what they had to him. She had died—but she had dismissed his memory long, long before that. . . .

When his mother should die, when Cecily too was gone, and he, Stephen, a numb old man, sat in that wicker chair by the fire-place, he would be thinking of Kate, and even then in a heart anaesthetized by age there would be a dull throb of pain that he had not meant enough to her, that she had forgotten him long, long before she died. . . .

"Sophie doesn't know what unhappiness is, Jay," he said. "Sophie's young. Only we old ones know."

The old doctor looked at his friend curiously and his eyes went back to the daughter.

"You may be right," he said slowly. "Perhaps . . . perhaps . . .

For Lynn and Sophie there was no need for conversation. Content stole over Sophie the moment Lynn took her in his arms for the dance. There was reassuring strength in his shoulders and hands, strength that enveloped and protected her. Here was safety, safety from loneliness and from that Sophie one did not know, that tormented other self who sobbed at night for terrifying unknown things. In this strength there must lie permanent peace.

That he belonged to her there could be no doubt, for he ignored everyone else. He did not trouble to pay her compliments. Was it not compliment enough that he had chosen her out of all the women in the world?—that with Anna Stacey's hand tugging at his sleeve he did not turn his eyes away from Sophie? Somehow they accepted each other as a destined mate. Sophie Truelove and Lynn Hamilton. They were hushed with the peace each brought to the other.

Anna Stacey laughed with the men and pretended not to see Lynn after that. Oh, she prayed, for the gift of being cruel to him and to that woman, that woman who possessed the things Anna herself had yearned for. But all her life things had been torn from Anna—money, beauty, charm, lovers—and now the husband she might have had. . . . Very well, from now on she would tear things from life. She would be as cruel as life itself—bitterly savagely cruel. She only wept because of her puniness, because her hands were so small. . . .

It soothed her to be vicious to George Truelove, who was so plainly attracted by her—great clumsy creature that he was. Through him she strove to hit at Sophie. By making him appear foolish, she would humiliate the sister. But George himself only stared with added admiration at her when she jibed at him. Her very sarcasm charmed him. He was fascinated too, by her tiny high-heeled feet flying about the dance floor. He had never seen such amazing feet—small elfin feet, they would leave in the snow a mark no deeper than a fox's footprint. For him there was an exotic lure in her anemic face and meager body, contrasting as it did with the buxom Bessies of the neighborhood. There was an odd disturbance in his bosom now, a puzzling discontent that he could not classify, he who had always been comfortably serene and untroubled by desire. For George yearning was a new experience and he was helpless. He could not have described it as a desire for the little schoolteacher, because he did not yet recognize his emotion. He only knew that looking at Anna Stacey made him discontented, and that her flaunted preference for Hart Purvis bothered him incontinently.

Dance after dance Anna refused George. She would show everyone what she thought of the Trueloves. When the end of a dance found her standing beside Lynn and Sophie she smiled vaguely past Lynn and allowed herself to be introduced half a dozen times by her escort to the bewildered Sophie. No, she had not met Miss Truelove before. . . . When out of the corner of her eye she saw the adoration in Lynn's attitude toward Sophie she could not bear to be near them but would hurry away.

At twelve the musicians stopped and the guests followed Mrs. Hamilton's panting lead downstairs. Dishes clattered, glasses tinkled, Jenny and the serving girls rushed frantically from kitchen to parlor with plates heaped at once with chicken, pickles, salad, jellies, crullers, tarts and pie. Young men bashful during the dance took on bold airs after an enormous supper and a few glasses of cherry bounce. Tom Hamilton presided with ever-increasing joviality at the punch bowl.

"Won't be long, eh, Anna?" he shouted, clapping a hand on the schoolteacher's shoulder. He nodded toward the young men. "If it isn't Hart there, it'll be one of the Coles' boys or Truelove over there. Think of it, Anna, three handsome men for you to choose from!"

Anna's shoulder wriggled from under her host's hand.

"You needn't worry," she said coldly. "Your Trueloves don't interest me—not if I was fifty and still an old maid."

George reddened to the ears and all the men guffawed. But her very bitterness increased her mystery. He didn't understand it, and it made her more provocative than ever. He wanted to say things to her but he was speechless before her venom. He wanted to be near her and have her smile at him in the twisted knowing way she smiled at Hart Purvis. He wanted her to look at him with the gaunt eagerness she looked after Lynn Hamilton. The thought of her went wriggling maddeningly through his veins. He wanted—yes, he wanted to put his hands on her skinny little shoulders and shake her. Shake her and overpower her with his strong muscles so that he wouldn't be afraid of her anymore.

Lynn drove Sophie home in his cutter. He was going on from there to spend the night at his uncle's farm near the Ridge. All the long drive home he said scarcely a word, yet their silence seemed to bind them more completely than any speech. The thing between them was settled. As they drew up in the driveway of the Truelove farm, Lynn peered down at Sophie, bundled up to the chin in fur.

"Do you remember that day in town," he asked, "coming out of the post office?"

"Yes," answered Sophie in a low voice.

"I've thought about you ever since," he went on steadily. "I wasn't sure, then, but now. . . ."

Sophie sat very still and did not look at him. Lynn was silent a moment, fingering the reins in his hand.

"You're not like any other woman, Sophie," he said presently. "I was a little afraid of you. I don't know. . . . It's dangerous for a man to fall in love with a woman like you. . . . Seems as if it would be harder to make you happy . . . I was afraid. . . ."

The horse had stopped at the side entrance of the house. The lamp that Mrs. Truelove had left burning in the dining room flung a spear of light across the driveway. The snow shimmered under its rays. Sophie waited motionless for Lynn to go on, but he said no more. He leaped out of the sleigh, and held out his hands to help her. She wanted to say to him, "I'm not different from other women. You needn't fear. Oh, my dear—my dear—it would be so easy for you to make me happy." But instead she stood on the step with her gloved hand still resting in his. Words would not come to her, used as she was to guarding them. She only smiled at him a little wistfully.

"Good bye, Sophie," he said.

He dropped her hands abruptly and leaped into the sleigh.

"Don't be afraid—don't be afraid of me," Sophie cried after him softly.

Lynn leaned toward her.

"What did you say?"

Sophie put her muff up to her face.

"I only said good-night," she said, and went into the house.

Early in the spring Mary Cecily and her three-year old came up from Crawford County for their yearly visit. Mary Cecily would help her mother with all of the spring sewing. This year there would be more than ever, for Lotta's three must have new outfits. Lotta had sent the money for the material and asked her sister-in-law to keep the children until fall, for she said, "I am going through a crisis in my own life and have no strength to give them. . . ."

The sewing machine was up in the attic and the bolts of gingham, denim and batiste were piled on a long pine table. By the time Mary Cecily left in June those bolts would be magically transformed into piles of aprons, small jumpers, blue shirts for the men, a flowered silk in ruffled tiers for Sophie, a lace-trimmed muslin to be worn to church, some simple muslins for Mary Cecily, Grandma and Cecily. There was to be another costume for Sophie, too, a white broadcloth that Mrs. Truelove thought of as Sophie's traveling suit, for the honeymoon.

"Don't let Sophie or the men know," Cecily had written to Mary Cecily a few days before she arrived, "but I think we had best fit out Sophie completely for this spring. Tom Hamilton's boy has been coming over every Sunday for a long time and you know Sophie well enough to know she wouldn't see him unless she meant to take him. We were afraid she'd never find any man to suit her, and while I cannot bear to have her go away from home, I know that she must because it isn't good for women to stay single purposely. Mind now, that you don't mention this to her when you come, because Sophie doesn't think I know."

Mary Cecily was not likely to speak of it, for she was an abstracted soul, and seldom remembered such details as her mother had presented to her. She was a tall girl, with a light fragile body and pale transparent hands. Her eyes were a brilliant blue and her thin white face under its ash-gold hair constantly wore an expression of rapt expectancy. There was a ghostly quality about Mary Cecily. Encountering her as she fluttered about the house one was sure that a mortal touch would cause her to vanish into air.

It was strange that her ethereal charm should have captivated the stocky, surly Bert Lysinger. Stranger still that this stolid man should have satisfied Mary Cecily's romantic ideal. Yet they had been married several years and never once on her annual visits home did Mary Cecily appear anything but contented. It was true that Bert had refused her one great thing. He would not buy her a piano, in spite of his increasing prosperity, but, as her mother told her, she could get enough music on her long visits home, practicing on the old square piano in the parlor.

Mary Cecily did not play the piano more than fairly well, nor did she know much of music. She would sit at the tinkly old piano in the somber Truelove parlor and play through a hymn-book, sometimes fumbling over chords, but always with a fanatic absorption. Sophie could not remember her older sister apart from her piano playing. When Sophie was only eleven, she had stood in the hall outside the parlor, puzzled and vaguely unhappy over the endless monotonous rhythm of Mary Cecily's playing. Presently the parlor door would open and a radiant, rapt Mary Cecily would emerge, brushing past the little girl as though she were air.

Even sharing the same room as they had for years there was no bond between these two. The boys were as like as brothers could be, but Mary Cecily and little Sophie were two strangers who had nothing to say to each other, whose silences were not shared moods but oceans dividing them. Between Mary Cecily and her mother, however, there lay a quiet love that made no effort at understanding. Mary Cecily was more Mills than Truelove, said the mother, and the Mills were still, safe folks who said little and seldom laughed.

Sophie and Lynn knew now that they would marry. Lynn had asked nothing, but one Sunday in April he had taken her down to his uncle's three hundred acres by the Ridge woods and said quietly, "We will build here."

Sophie had answered, "We'll have a white house with green shutters."

It was a relief to know, to have those old uncertainties eased. Lynn loved her—then this was what she had always sought. Life would be so beautifully simple. There would be no darkness, no frenzied wonderings as to what *was* one's desire, what *did* one seek, for here was the answer in Lynn's deep, shining love. This was what she had been questing all her life.

There was the night he had first kissed her.

It was the beginning of the spring, and roads were good enough for the farmers to drive to church again. Lynn had driven her over to the Ridge Church for the evening service. They had stayed to talk to the Coles' girls. Then, in the light of a young April moon they had driven home along the river road. They were silent. Beyond the edge of the village was the old cemetery, and Lynn's horse slowed up in passing with instinctive reverence.

But in the midst of the night hush the graveyard was alive with whispering and snickers, and over the black graves young bodies writhed in love. About the cemetery was a fringe of empty buggies, their horses nibbling at the myrtle on the monuments. Voices a few minutes ago lusty in the church choir now whispered amorously in the shadow of tombs. From a buggy at the foot of the hill stepped a girl who was unmistakably Bessie. With her was the barber from the Ridge. They went into the graveyard gate. Just inside, the girl stumbled over a headstone and burst out laughing. . . .

Shame flooded Sophie. These graveyard lovers, they could not know what love was. They could not know that love was silence and understanding.

Sophie found herself shaking with nameless horror. She put a hand on Lynn's sleeve.

"Lynn, please—" she appealed half sobbing, "love is not that— we know, don't we?"

Lynn put his arm about her.

"Yes, Sophie," he said, "we know. Oh, Sophie . . ."

Abruptly he dropped the reins. He took her face gently in his two hands and kissed her lips. Sophie closed her eyes. Lynn was strong and dear. He would keep their love high above this beast that hung over tombstones. He would keep their love a shining, starry thing, a rare and special charm against evil.

Sophie said nothing to her mother or sister, and knowing her they asked no questions. Cecily welcomed Lynn every Sunday with an understanding warmth, and Grandma Truelove's eyes filled when she saw him look at Sophie. Privately they talked of the wedding.

"You don't know how glad I am that it is a boy like Lynn." Cecily Truelove said to Mary Cecily. "The men *will* keep saying how Sophie is like her Aunt Lotta and I've always been afraid. . . ."

Cecily did not explain what she feared, nor did her older daughter understand what she meant. But she nodded, sympathetically.

One twilight Grandma Truelove and Sophie sat by the fire while in the adjoining room Mary Cecily played the piano. Sophie had looked into the fire for a long time. Her grandmother's old eyes were upon her steadily, her knitting idle in her lap.

"Will you marry him, Sophie?" she asked softly.

"I think so," Sophie whispered.

"You will be happy with him, Sophie?" the old woman asked again.

"I think so," repeated Sophie.

She had a sudden longing to ask that knowing old woman for some of her wisdoms, some of the answers she had found.

"That is what I want, isn't it?" she begged.

The old woman picked up her knitting and a veil came subtly between them.

"Marriage? Of course," she said, and then almost to herself. "I—think so."

The piano playing had stopped and Mary Cecily stood in the doorway.

"Marriage doesn't make any difference," she said in her soft gentle voice. "Marriage doesn't touch you—it doesn't touch you at all, do you see? You go on being alone—no matter what—do you see?"

Sophie saw Mary Cecily that instant as a totally new person. This was not the stranger who had accidentally been conceived in the same womb as herself, this was truly her own sister. It was the first time Sophie had ever recognized that kinship. She stared at the older girl.

"You mean it has nothing to do with what you really want . . . ." she asked. "Then it doesn't matter?"

Mary Cecily's eyes were gleaming with a faraway light. She leaned against the doorway lightly.

"It doesn't matter," she repeated. "It doesn't touch you, does it, Grandmother?"

The old woman bent her head over her knitting.

"It *should* make a woman happy," she evaded. It was not right for women to ask other women questions. It was not right for women to wonder. It was right that women should suffer for themselves. It was right that women should bear their own secrets.

She did not speak to Sophie again about marriage, nor did Mary Cecily. But Sophie knew and feared in her heart that what Mary Cecily had said was true . . . that even in Lynn's arms she would be desolate . . . that in the white house with the green shutters she would go on longing for unknown things.

Men were strange and stupid, Cecily Truelove thought. They lived under the same roof, sat at the same table, slept in the same beds with women, and yet dwelt in another world, belonged to another race. Here were four women who had known since the night of the Hamilton party months ago that Sophie and Lynn Hamilton would marry. Yet the men who shared the same roof and could have known the same thing had no inkling of it until Sophie herself told them.

Men were like that. A woman had no more language in common with them than she had with the farm cattle. It was small wonder that a husband and wife should spend every evening of a long winter before the fireplace without exchanging a word. How could they talk? They had no common tongue. Looking at one thing they did not see the same thing nor hear the same sounds. Men did not look, men did not listen. They were creatures who gave one babies and for this one knelt to them. But all her knowledge and all her questionings a woman must hide in herself for men were not made for knowledge or under-standing. They could not comprehend those things a woman knew. There was no tongue that could translate them to his for-eign reason.

Facts they understood. When Sophie's engagement had be-come a fact, then they talked of it. But the thing had not occurred to them before. Men saw black and white. Women saw all the degrees of gray between those two, but there was no use talking of it to men. They had only eyes with which to see.

The marriage would take place in the fall, Sophie and Lynn had said. By that time the house on Lynn's uncle's farm would be finished and meantime Stephen and Sophie would pick furniture from a city catalogue. There would be a huge wedding on the farm, and Trueloves and Mills from all over Ohio would come for it as they had to Mary Cecily's wedding seven years before. Sophie would wear an ivory satin wedding dress with a long train and Grandmother Truelove's own bridal lace would be her veil.

Cecily looked at her daughter sometimes with a little puzzled frown. For weeks before her own wedding she had walked in a magic sleep, star-eyed and exultant at the promise of life-long happiness. But Sophie went about the house exactly as she had before Lynn had come into her life—silent, enigmatical, reserved. When Lynn was there she glowed subtly. Already she was far removed from her mother. She belonged to her new life. But how calmly she accepted that change, thought Cecily, as though she were merely fulfilling a destiny of which she had always been aware.

As for Sophie there were nights when she knelt at her bedroom window looking out over the moonlit fields and pressing her hands against her head to still the strumming in her brain. She was going to marry Lynn, going to live in a beautiful cold white house with green shutters, going to belong to the only man whose face she had ever cherished in her mind. This was what women waited for. This was what they were born for. She was going to marry Lynn. She would lie in his arms at night, as Bessie did in the arms of her vulgar lovers, and her proud beauty would be defiled—that terror that had kept her awake and shuddering for so many long nights would be realized. . . . And the shutters of the beautiful cold white house would be closed and no one would know that Sophie Truelove had yielded to monstrous degradations. The shutters of the white house would be locked and no one would know that the bride had fled. No one would know that she was a wanton, dancing in the graveyard with goat-faced men. For it would never be Lynn who defiled her. Even with his face above her it would be a pageant of dreadful monsters who devoured her.

Sophie Truelove was afraid. She sat at the window, her black hair sweeping the sill, and despair shook her for the things that must happen—the things that even the bright armor of Lynn's love could not keep from her.

Sophie stayed home with Vera while the rest of the family drove Mary Cecily to her train, for Vera had triumphantly succumbed to tonsillitis.

"Don't forget to turn down the wick of the hall lamp," Cecily said, leaning from the spring wagon for these last minute admonitions. "And we won't be back till ten o'clock, so be sure to give Vera her tonic. Doctor Gardiner promised to send over a new bottle as soon as he could."

Sophie stood in the door, holding the lamp high so Mary Cecily's telescope could be safely strapped on. Then with a final quavering good-bye from the weeping Robert, the wagon rolled away and Sophie went back into the house.

Upstairs Grandma Truelove and Vera slept. The last echo of the wagon wheels died away and a creeping silence descended over the farm. Sophie tried to ignore it. She picked up her sewing and sat down under the table lamp humming softly. But she mocked at herself for trying to cover with her light voice the voices of silence. Lamps that had been cheerful when other people shared their light now flickered waywardly as though they were afraid. The wind blew in the curtains and their motion made shadows flutter on the wall.

Sophie sat for a long time trying to dismiss the sense of foreboding unaccountably stealing over her. She had never been afraid of any living thing. Her father had said she was the most fearless woman he had ever known. He could not know that a woman could handle a gun as well as a man and yet be afraid of her own thoughts.

She would be glad when she was in that white house with Lynn. He would not let her have fears. He would never be afraid. He would teach her to be as brave as he was. His deep cold strength would be her refuge. Through marriage a woman gained peace. Her mother had. All the Truelove women. And yet . . . Sophie found herself moving toward the dark parlor. She groped for the table—for the album beneath it. Where was the lamp? The matches? The quiet of this house seemed suddenly unbearable. The darkness was furnished with dangling masks, with sighs, and with waiting silences. Sophie fumbled with a match, struck it with unsteady fingers. The thick pages of the album flicked against each other under her hands . . . Her mother's face stared wistfully up at her. Here was her grandmother in a wedding veil—and Sophie recognized doubt in her eyes. Lotta here with a baby in her arms, looking beyond it with eager restless eyes . . . Ah, Lotta had found no peace in other women's consolations. Sophie closed the album but Lotta remained outside, a shadow on the door, a shudder in the window curtain, a thing to warn her, Sophie thought, that a woman could wander forever without knowing her goal, without knowing how to name her desire. Here in the dark parlor with the Truelove women it was foolish to think Lynn's house could imprison an echo, a cloud, or a west wind, and these were the things a lost woman could be. . . . Sophie pushed the album under the table and blew out the lamp. Upstairs Vera coughed and Sophie's heart stopped at this sudden sound. She backed slowly out of the room, afraid of the breathing darkness. She closed the parlor door, but even the bright dining room had grown strange. . . . Vera coughed again and Sophie, anxious for any companionship, hurried upstairs. She lit a candle on the bureau of the children's room and saw that Vera was awake.

"Do you think I'll die, Cousin Sophie?" Vera asked.

"Hush—you must sleep," Sophie said and straightened the covers on the bed. She thought, "Someday I will have children of my own. Then I will be happy."

Downstairs the clock struck nine—or was it ten? Sophie listened. She heard the creak of the front gate and then footsteps on the porch. Now there was a knock at the door, but Sophie could not move. She wanted to call out but her tongue refused words. Then she was at the bedroom window, calling out, "Come in," and the downstairs door opened. Steps sounded hesitantly across the floor and a man's voice at the foot of the staircase said, "I've brought the medicine." Sophie stood in Vera's doorway. She could not take a step because of her ridiculous sense of fear, and yet it could only be Fred Tompkins, the doctor's hired man. She commanded herself to speak.

"Do you mind bringing it up, Fred?" she asked. The next moment she saw that it was not Fred. She had an impression of bulk and coal-black hair and something familiar in the strong Indian slant of his face.

"I frightened you, I'm sorry." His voice had a warm, rich color that tinged the air. "My father wanted a prescription to reach you tonight and I brought it over."

Now she remembered a market day in town and the rider of the black horse. She felt color unreasonably coming into her cheeks.

"I suppose you are Jerome Gardiner," she said. "I have heard my father speak of you."

She allowed him to follow her into the room. Vera was sitting up in bed, her eyes fixed first on Sophie and then on Jerome.

"I have heard of you, too," the man smiled. "I have even seen you one day in town. You could hardly be forgotten."

Sophie did not answer. She was bewildered by the whirl of excitement that went through her at this stranger's voice, at the curious hint of sorrow in his eyes. Standing in shadow he seemed faintly unreal, as if he were one of the presences the album had released a while back in the dark parlor. She could almost see Lotta behind him—but no, those were Vera's eyes. . . . Sophie gripped the back of a chair. He leaned over the foot of the bed, still smiling at her. . . . Sophie smiled, too, an odd, frozen little smile. The silence of the low-ceiled room was charged with strange currents. Sophie took a deep breath. It was because the night had been waiting for some calamity that this man's coming seemed significant. He was nothing really. Only Jerome Gardiner . . . Yet Sophie stood motionless and pale in the swaling candle-light, and her hand trembled on the chair. Vera leaned back on her pillows.

"Father said the child is not so ill," said Jerome Gardiner. He did not look at the small invalid at all. "But you are to give her this medicine for another week."

It was his voice, that rich husky voice, that terrified her, Sophie thought. Its vibrations caressed her as though he knew her charm, just as his dark brooding eyes caressed her, just as his great frame dominated the little room and her with a hidden force. Blood swam in Sophie's head. She could not look away from his intent eyes and in that moment when no word was spoken something black and tragic welled in Sophie's heart. This strange man was a part of the night's terror. To Sophie's taut nerves it seemed that he had been stalking for a thousand nights in the shadow of her thoughts—waiting to be admitted to her reality. She could remember that day in town when something in his eyes as he rode past had compelled her to look after him.

"It's only Doctor Gardiner's son," she told herself. "He means nothing to me . . . nothing. Why does he stay? Why does he look at me? . . . I must say something. I must say . . ."

Seconds were dangerous when their eyes held each other so. . . . And this panting silence between them as if in another instant one or the other would leap. She must break the spell. All she need do was to take two steps and she would be free of it. All she need do was to say, "Good-night, Mr. Gardiner. . . ." If he would only speak, since she could not . . . They had stood there for a century—or was it only a moment? . . . And here she was weak and shaken while he had suddenly pressed his hand over his eyes as if to shut out a white brilliance he could not endure.

Vera moved impatiently but Sophie had forgotten her. She had forgotten the vial of medicine clutched in her hand. She knew only that her breast ached with tears and that this stranger's voice and eyes held a dreadful enchantment she dared not break. The air thrummed between them.

"Good-night—and thank you," she murmured and took a step forward. Jerome walked over and opened the door. Their hands almost touched but drew hastily apart. She followed him to the dark hallway and saw him rest one hand for a moment on the railing, the other hand over his eyes.

"Good-night, Jerome Gardiner," she said again and did not know her hand was stretched toward him until he had bent swiftly and kissed it twice. Then he hurried down the stairs and the front door closed softly.

Sophie's knees shook. She stared down the dark hallway in a daze. Here was the dark dream, here was the dreadful thing she had known would come to her . . . this pounding in her head . . . this throbbing in her loins. . . . If their lips had once touched they could never have freed themselves. . . . They were not free even now.

She put her clenched hand—the one Jerome had kissed—to her mouth and her teeth sank into the knuckles.

"Cousin Sophie!" Vera called.

She leaned against the wall shivering.

II

$\mathcal{D}$OWN BY THE WOODS on the Ridge road the white house was growing. Every day Lynn and his men were working on it. It was not a bride-and-groom cottage, but a square, spacious house for a family, the sort of home Hamiltons built for their brides. People from all over Ashton County stopped to admire its solid lines.

"The finest lumber he could get," farmers told each other. "The Hamiltons are like that. Build for their great-grandchildren."

Girls driving by with their beaux said wistfully, "That's the place Lynn Hamilton is bringing his bride."

The men looked at the house and sighed, remembering that once Sophie Truelove had smiled at them.

One Sunday morning a creaky but still respectable buggy drawn by a plump horse stepping with the majesty of distinguished years drew up before the house. No one was in sight, and after a moment three women got out of the buggy. Two of them were dressed identically in starched saffron gowns, black velvet ribbons fluttering, high saffron kid shoes, black lace mitts, and rather startled-looking leghorn hats. The other woman was small and restless, and wore a sagging white muslin gown with a broad apple-green sash. The three picked their way across the upturned earth, poking their ruffled parasols in the sprouting lawn, and staring avidly at the nearly completed building. It was still unpainted, and there were heaps of lumber piled in the back yard and against the remote new stables.

"It is almost as big as the Truelove's house," said Lucy Anderson. "I mean before they built the wing. Sophie will have to keep help."

"They've built it for children," said Sara.

"Maybe she'll be like Dora Hamilton and not have any," said Anna Stacey softly. "Some women are like that."

The three women contemplated this thought with some pleasure for a moment.

"I always say it's dangerous to build before you're really married," said Lucy, "So many times the marriage doesn't come off."

"That's true," Anna agreed pointedly.

She ran up the steps of the porch, ahead of the other two. She hated to be with them always. As if she were being groomed for the same fate as theirs! Yellow withered old virgins! She despised herself for coming out with them this morning, for wanting as badly as they did to see the house where those two would live. She would like to have kept apart, to have said to them indifferently, "Only old maids are interested in young couples' houses. *I* shall have one of my own someday."

But she had said nothing. She had followed eagerly. That meant that she too would be an old maid. She would teach the Ridge school forever and live with the Anderson girls and people would point to their house saying, "Three old maids live there all alone."

Anna's lips were bleeding from her nervous gnawing. The three had come into the kitchen with its smell of fresh plastering and new lumber. The Sunday sun, always a little paler than on other days, shone through the windows across the bare, paint-spattered floor.

Lucy and Sara fluttered about examining the molding, the pantry, the high cupboards, the alcove where the stove would stand.

"She will cook for him here," breathed Lucy. Sara nodded.

Anna drew a sharp breath. She was an old maid. Coming with Lucy and Sara made her one. Riding over the country to peer in newlyweds' windows. Horrible!

Sara straightened up and sent a meaning look to her sister, cocking her head questioningly.

"Well—shall we look upstairs?" she asked brightly.

Lucy tittered self-consciously.

"Why, I think we might," she said.

They lifted their saffron skirts high above their skinny old legs and mounted the staircase. Anna looked after them, fierce loathing in her eyes. She shouldn't be curious. These things should all be an accepted part of her future. Of course she would have a house as Sophie Truelove had. Of course she would have a husband of her choosing. Of course there would be babies.

"Coming, Ann?" called Lucy from the top of the stairs.

"No," said Anna stubbornly.

But her feet were on the sawdust-strewn staircase as she spoke. She followed the two old women down the hallway.

"Five bedrooms," counted Lucy breathlessly. "I wonder which . . ."

Sara was opening and shutting doors intently. "It's usually the corner one," she said abstractedly, "for the two exposures. Ah . . ."

Undoubtedly this was the bridal chamber. A great sunny room with a larger closet than the others and the woodwork already painted white. There was a cedar box, too, built under the window. A bride would see to that.

Sara and Lucy stood stock-still in the middle of the room, their eyes glowing. Anna watched them, despising them, and despising herself for following them. She belonged to this room. She might have won Lynn Hamilton. He had smiled at her, he had been kind from the very first day she had gone to his house—he had been sorry when she left for the Andersons'. If it were not for Sophie Truelove, he would belong to Anna Stacey. . . . So this was to be their bedroom.

"I want to go," she said harshly. "Supposing someone should find us here, snooping about like—like old maids."

Sara's eyes lowered and she sped a lightning glance at her sister and then at Anna.

"Well—aren't we?" she tittered.

"No!" Anna cried. "I'm not an old maid! I'm not like you. I won't be!"

"You're twenty-seven, dear—almost thirty," soothed Lucy. "After all we don't mind so much, do we, Sara? We have our pleasures."

"Watching other people," snapped Anna.

She went downstairs again, hate seething inside her. They dared not say she was one of them. They dared not. Yet—they had. She shivered at the peck-peck of their voices behind her.

"Shall we drive on to church?" asked Lucy sweetly.

Anna, without answering, went out the kitchen door, leaving them ah-ing over a newly discovered preserve closet. She saw that rosebushes had already been transplanted to the back yard and a trellis had been built for grapes. It ran from the back door to the little cottage where old Will Carter, the Hamilton's hired man, was going to live.

Anna sniffed. Tobacco smoke was in the air. A man—perhaps Lynn Hamilton himself—was somewhere about, sneering at them for their spinsters' curiosity. Anna looked around sharply. Then she saw that a man was leaning against the lumber pile, near the trelliswork, smoking idly. There was a faintly foreign air about him, the distinction of cities. She stepped on a loose board. He turned and she saw a lean olive-skinned face with smoldering black eyes.

"Why, Mr. Gardiner!" exclaimed Anna. "What are you doing here?"

Jerome tapped his pipe against the wood, and looked down at the schoolteacher's pinched eager face.

"Interested in architecture," he answered smoothly.

Anna fancied something mocking behind his words that made her redden.

"I came with them—" she nodded toward the flutter of yellow skirts on the side porch. "I didn't want to come. You see I'm— I'm not interested in architecture."

She was angry at the hinted knowledge in his dark eyes. He had watched them going over the house. He thought she was like *them*. Anna was furious at having provided this superior person with cause for amusement.

"I doubt if you're so interested in architecture," she stabbed blindly, "Isn't it more likely you wanted to see where Sophie Truelove is going to live?"

She was immediately sorry she had raged. Her weak jibes would probably amuse him too. Well, let him smile. But glancing swiftly up at him Anna saw that he was not smiling, that his eyes seemed blacker than before, his jaw more set.

"Anna . . . ! Ann!"

Jerome pulled his soft hat over his eyes abruptly.

"My respects to your friends," he said, "I'm going this way and would rather not talk to them. Good-day."

Anna watched him striding across the east meadow, and her mouth twisted in a curious smile.

"Was Will Carter back there?" demanded Sara, settling herself once more in the buggy, her skirts lifted carefully in the back to avoid crumpling.

"Yes," said Anna.

"Fancy being married and living in that house!" said Lucy. "Fancy!"

She picked up the reins daintily—she was the oldest and always drove—in her lace-mittened hands, and clicked convincingly. Dobbin vibrated for a moment with thoughts of motion. Presently to his secret astonishment his legs began to move.

Summer trailed over the fields. Young colts leaped in the meadows behind proud snorting mares. Calves, wobbly and frightened, nosed casual cows. Vats of new-made soap were lined against the summer kitchens and the air was chopped with the click of thrashers in far-off fields.

On the Truelove farm cherry trees blossomed and then were jeweled with fruit. The orchard was in perpetual song. Ladders slanted against the trees and when the men were not picking cherries Lotta's children might be seen performing perilous acrobatics on the rungs. Sometimes they were allowed to help in the picking, but the pails they brought to the kitchen door after a morning's labor were barely sprinkled with cherries, and their helpful efforts were invariably followed by a night of acute interior distress.

In the kitchen Bessie stood over the stove, her face and arms steamed to the color of ham, while she stirred kettles of boiling fruit juice with a huge wooden spoon. Cecily and Grandmother Truelove sat on low stools with pails on either side of them and pitted cherries. The air was drenched with the hot sweet piercing smell. Flies clung to the screen door in an ecstasy of anticipation.

Sophie stood at the long table washing the fruit jars and jelly glasses. Her dark blue starched cambric, open at the throat brought out deceptive blue lights in her black hair, deepened the color of her eyes and the ivory pallor of her skin.

"Sophie will be putting up in her own kitchen next year," said Bessie, dabbing a towel at her dripping forehead. "Maybe taking prizes at the fair. 'Mrs. Lynn Hamilton, Ashton Ridge, Quince Jelly. Blue Ribbon.' Ha, ha!"

"Our women never make good quince jelly," said Grandmother Truelove proudly.

"The Mills women have always been famous for their jellies," said Cecily, "Sophie might take from my side of the family."

"No, she won't," said Grandmother serenely. "She's all Truelove."

The two women mentally locked horns for an instant. Grandmother Truelove's eyes filled. She had been insulted. Cecily had dared to say that one of her grandchildren—indeed her own dear Sophie—was a Mills. Cecily was horrid to her, a poor old woman. She was too old to be sitting here pitting cherries anyway. Too old to be in this hot kitchen. She should be petted and humored and made much of. People should make her cool drinks on these warm days and fan her with the great palm-leaf fan. No, sir, she would not sit in this kitchen any longer.

"Are you sure you aren't overdoing?" asked Cecily. "Don't you think, Mother, that you'd better go and rest?"

"Certainly not," said Grandmother Truelove. "I'm not in my grave, you know, Cecily. Not yet."

"At least let Sophie make you a nice lemonade," urged Cecily. "Sophie, run down and bring some fresh water from the spring."

"I don't want any lemonade," coldly retorted the old woman. How cruel of Cecily to make her feel old and pampered and useless!

"Yes, sir, Sophie'll be Mrs. Hamilton before we know it," said Bessie jovially. She sent a sly glance at the slim girl near the table.

She was older than Bessie but she didn't know about men the way Bessie did. She might be a beauty as folks said, but she didn't know about men. Bessie knew. She smiled with secret tolerance, and thought of the barber on the Ridge.

"October tenth," said Cecily, musingly. "October tenth. That's the wedding day, you know, Mother. October tenth."

"As if I didn't know that," muttered Grandmother.

Sophie's hands among the glasses were still.

"I've changed the date," she said.

"What!" Cecily was horrified. "Bad luck to postpone it," admonished Grandmother.

"I'm not postponing it." Sophie bent her head and a faint flush stole into her cheeks. "I want to be married before then. You see our house will be ready next month. I thought . . . we thought . . ."

She could sense her mother's amazement without turning around. Girls should be shy and reluctant about their marriage. It was scarcely decent to want to hasten the date.

"Why shouldn't we be married next month?" Sophie went on in a desperate effort to be casual. "Why couldn't we be married on the afternoon of the Truelove Reunion? The day after the County Fair closes."

"The whole family would be here for it, then," reflected Cecily. "Uncle Charles and the Cincinnati Trueloves and the Michigan branch. They always come for Reunion."

"And maybe Lotta" suggested Grandmother.

"I want Aunt Lotta to be here for my wedding," Sophie said. It seemed to her that Aunt Lotta was the only person in the world who could help her to solve things; and yet she was vaguely afraid of the solution Lotta might offer.

"I think it's a very good idea," observed Grandmother Truelove. "The folks will all be here for the Reunion anyway."

Cecily resumed her cherry pitting thoughtfully. She would write and tell Mary Cecily tonight.

Sophie recognized her silence as agreement and breathed relief. She must marry Lynn quickly before this confusion in her brain drove her mad. If she were married to him she would not think of anyone else. She would not be alone in the night, tormented with a desire to see Jerome Gardiner again. She would belong all to Lynn and Jerome Gardiner would be only a dark, heavy-eyed ghost. When Lynn was with her his shadow faded away, and Lynn was all-enveloping. But she was too often frightened by the memory of one night and the strange excitement of a dark man's presence. She dreaded that hour of night when her father rose from the card table, stretched his great frame and yawned, "Well, girls, ready for bed?" and George locked the doors, and Cecily helped Grandmother to bed.

That was the beginning of terror. Then the comfortable day sounds faded into the walls, the curtains, the beams, and there was only the pompous ticking of the tall mantel clock, the creaking of stairs, the tapping of wind-shaken maple branches against the windows. Then Sophie lay huddled in her bed, her closed fingers pressed against her eyes. She would not remember. She would not dare remember. She would think of Lynn. Blue—ice-blue eyes. Standing in front of the post office that first day . . . taking her so gently in his arms as though he feared his strength might crush her. And then . . . then the branches brushed her window again to remind her that night was out there waiting to take her, and her heart began to pound and weakness came over her. A dark man became a hot breathing presence beside her in the quivering shadow.

Sophie turned and buried her face in the pillow but he was there. Doom was behind his sad smile and before his eyes Sophie's body swelled and blackness swirled over her. She was Bessie. She laughed a little as she stumbled over a gravestone.

Lotta was coming for the Fair.

Cecily prepared a smile for her coming and flourished it like a bright flag when Stephen or the children talked of her visit. Lotta had not been on the farm in twenty years but the county had not forgotten her. People discussed breathlessly her return. The Truelove's black sheep was coming home to ask forgiveness, they said. They asked Cecily—on her every other Saturday marketing—if Lotta would bring her husband with her, and what was her name now? Was it true that she had a salon hung in black velvet with a crystal ball and East Indian servants—and that the President himself consulted her concerning his private and political affairs?

Cecily would distressfully evade their questions, ask after Aunt Hannah's rheumatism or Emma's children, and hurry on to the refuge of the market wagon. Oh, she was afraid of Lotta's coming. Lotta would remind Stephen of disturbing things, and he would sit in his chair out under the maple with his pipe gone out in his hand, and not know. He would forget that she, Cecily, was there in the little willow rocker beside him. She would put her hand remindingly on his knee, but he would look in the wind's face as if there he saw the old romance that Lotta's restless spirit conjured up for him. Lotta under the roof again would stir ancient fires, because Lotta was romance—Lotta had run with whatever breeze had blown. She would recall to Stephen the big blonde woman who had laughed with him, and he would withdraw into the walled loneliness that Cecily beat against in vain.

Lotta had written to Stephen: "There are things, Stephen, that one must do—things one cannot resist. I know it would be far wiser for me to stay away from Ashton. I was wretchedly unhappy there, and people still talk, I know. . . . But this summer I am impelled to come back, perhaps only for a day or two, perhaps only to remind myself of how unhappy I once was—but how much more unhappy than now."

She spoke of taking the children back to Washington with her, but at this news a loud wail went up from the three small Wintons.

"I don't think Mama ought to take us back, do you, Aunt Cecily?" Lois demanded. "It will be so lonesome for you without us."

There would be emptiness, agreed Cecily, as well as relief in not having children to worry about. They were odd children, not at all lovable, yet a house needed children. They formed a buffer between herself and Grandmother Truelove. When they went, she would be left with nothing between herself and the old woman but their naked hatred. Cecily could remember that year she had come to this house a bride—how she had prayed each night for a baby, so that she need not be left an instant alone with Stephen's mother—Stephen's mother who despised her because she was little and frail when the Truelove women were all big, handsome women who commanded men. . . . No, she must never be left alone with her again—even after all these years.

"I think the country is really better for the children than Washington," she said quickly to Stephen. "Perhaps Lotta will let them stay. They—they were doing so nicely over at the Ridge school."

"I'm not going to Washington," Custer announced firmly.

His eldest sister gave him a look.

"Oh yes, indeed you are," she coldly informed him. "It's bad for you here because you've learned to swear from John. I'm going to tell Mama you said 'damn.' He stood in the middle of the granary, Uncle Stephen, and said 'damn, damn, DAMN,' to himself. I listened at the door. He's only five, too."

"Why!" gasped Cecily.

Custer was embarrassed and chagrined at having been observed in his secret rites. His thin sallow face became a deep red and he became very warm inside. He didn't want to look up from the rug, not because he had said damn, but because his sister had seen him pretending to be John.

"Tut, tut!" said Uncle Stephen.

Custer, much relieved at his uncle's preoccupation, wriggled out of the room. Once behind the door he caught his sister's eye and vigorously thumbed his nose. She lowered her eyes modestly.

"Of course Lotta may not come at all," said Cecily. "You remember she was going to come for Mary Cecily's wedding, and then at the last minute she never showed up at all. I shouldn't be a bit surprised if she didn't come."

"Lotta will come," was torn from Grandmother Truelove. Cruel, cruel Cecily to hint that she would not come. The baby, her lovely yellow-haired baby. Of course she would come.

"She'll come," said Vera positively. She closed her eyes and sniffed the air as if already it were charged with the excitement that always preceded her mother's entrances. Swish—swish— in an outside hall, and people suddenly stopping in their talk and men fingering their ties and women folding their hands, looking at each other. Swish—swish—little gusts of perfume and then the door opening and everyone saying "ah." . . . Vera was glad she was beautiful, too, like her mother. Someday she too would have a black velvet basque and silk petticoats and she would sit quietly for a long time while people bent forward and waited for her to speak, because her voice was lovely. She, yes, she would be a lady in furs in a carriage like those ladies who came to see her mother. Lois and Custer would be conveniently dead—here Vera brushed away a tear—so there would be no one to torment her. . . . Vera adjusted an imaginary pelisse about her shoulders and smiled a sad, enigmatic smile at Lois.

"Lotta will be surprised to find the children looking so well," said Cecily. She would not let them go. Stephen must not let them go away. She would not be alone day in and day out with that old woman by the fireplace. Nothing to talk about—only each other to think of—and Stephen always silent.

"Lotta will probably be willing to have them stay—at least until Christmas," said Stephen. He stroked his blonde beard and studied Lois's pointed smirking face as though he really were considering the problem of the children. But they were not in his thoughts. . . . He was thinking of the question he must ask Lotta when she came. If it was true that the stars knew everything, if it was true that certain persons—why not Lotta?—had the power to communicate with the dead, then might there not be some word Lotta could give to him, some message from Kate, a denial perhaps of what had seemed her indifference? . . . Men could not go on forever without knowing those things. They could not.

Stephen's hand clenched his pipe. Cecily stole a sidelong glance at him, saw that his pipe had gone out, saw the look in his eyes, and was aware of sounds coming from her suddenly unhappy mouth.

"Ancient of Days, who sitteth crowned in Glory. . . ." she sang in her quavering monotone.

One afternoon Sophie and her father sat in the dark musty parlor of the Gardiner home, waiting for the doctor to return from a call. They would have preferred to wait on the veranda, but the withered old housekeeper had ushered them with dignified re-proach into the room where formal calls should be made.

The parlor had been embalmed with its dead mistress fifteen years ago. In those fifteen years, thanks to the housekeeper's morbid loyalty, no conch shell or figurine had been changed on the black walnut whatnot, no antimacassar (filet with fringe) on the horsehair upholstery had been allowed to wrinkle. The air was still weighted, sanctified with the suggestion of embalming fluid, funeral wreaths, and the medicated tears of bereaved ones. Red plush curtains—moth-eaten and musty-hung in the windows, portieres of the same—caught up at one side with gold cords—in the doorways. Bulging pillows of velvet with lace medallions stood stiffly against chair legs. On a marble-topped oval table sat a glass-encased French clock supported by two leering gold nudes. The clock had never made any pretense of keeping time, but Hattie Gardiner used to think the little nymphs were so sweet.

Sophie sat on a horsehair sofa near the fern-filled window twisting her fingers and smoothing out the bouffant gaiety of her pink-flowered muslin. Under her drooping leghorn hat, her face looked pale and her eyes shadowed. She had feared to come into this house, yet when she had suggested waiting in the phaeton for her father to finish his talk—what had he to discuss with Dr. Gardiner, she wondered—he had brushed the thought aside. Of course the doctor would want to see Sophie. Of course she must come in. . . . Entering, she told herself she must think of it as only a house, not a place throbbing with the history of a certain man. He was back in Washington, she knew. There could be no danger of an encounter.

Out the window she could see Fred Tompkins galloping around the edge of the pasture on a sleek velvet thoroughbred. A group of boys—town boys, she thought—hung about the stable door as they did every year when Fred was grooming the horses for the Fair or the County Horse Show. . . . Jerome would come back then, but she would not see him. After all, he was nothing to her—not even a friend. Once she was married, he would not exist even in her mind. She would be free then to think always of Lynn as she had for those long months before he sought her. . . .

Opposite her in a carved cathedral chair sat Stephen Truelove. There were black bookshelves at his back—Sir Walter Scott in green, Miss Mulock's works in cherry, History of Medicine very suitably in black, "Childe Harolde," "Lucile," and even "Capitolas Peril"—acting as modulators from Dickens (complete) to Balzac (complete) to Sainte-Beuve (complete)—and then long unbroken stretches of Britannica, Bible Concordats, Thackeray, Shakespeare, Charles Lever, bound volumes of the *Living Age, Harper's Weekly,* and medical journals. The red and green façade presented by the bookshelves blurred into the black of the medical journals. Sophie, gazing at this somber spectacle, felt her emotions chloroformed, numbed, embalmed. Jerome Gardiner had never seemed farther away than here in the gloomy parlor of his own childhood home. Sophie smiled at the paradox of his burning aliveness and this mausoleum. Here was one place his spirit could not dominate.

There were footsteps in the hall and then the portieres parted for the doctor.

He pulled off his linen duster and looked about helplessly for a place to fling it. Defeated by the impregnable formality of the room he finally dashed into the adjoining room and came back relieved, twisting his white mustache. He sat down on the sofa beside Sophie, and glanced around the room cautiously.

"Della showed you in here, I suppose," he said. "She's very proud of it. Keeps it just the way it was before Hattie died. Insists on callers waiting in here, though when I'm here I take 'em out to the stable where we can be comfortable. A—a rather pretty room, though, don't you think? Hattie always thought so."

He sighed and looked longingly toward the window.

Stephen coughed.

"Lotta's coming back, Tom," he said abruptly. "Sophie and I were driving home from market and I thought we'd stop off and tell you. She'll be here around Reunion time—maybe for Sophie's wedding."

The doctor's face beamed.

"By George, that's good news, Stephen," he declared. "I wonder how the folks will take it. Is she separated from this last husband, do you know?"

"You never did get over Lotta, did you, Jay," Stephen commented with a wry smile. "She's fond of you, too. Always was. That's why I called on you." He got up and stood before the doctor. "Do you think it's wise for her to come back, here, Jay? Don't you think it would be better for me to write her not to come?"

"Wise?" repeated the doctor, "Of course it isn't wise or Lotta wouldn't have thought of it. Lotta's too old to start doing the things that are for the best."

Stephen began slowly pacing up and down the rose-strewn carpet, his gray-blonde head bent.

"I don't mean wise for Lotta," he said, "wise for the rest of us. I'm fond of Lotta. You know that. But she upsets me. She upsets everyone—people comfortable and fairly happy. She's a gadfly. I've been thinking of her, and I swear I'm too old to be reminded of—of unhappy things. Lotta does that to you, somehow. Reminds you of the things you might have done. . . . What do you think?"

The doctor looked at Stephen thoughtfully and then his glance strayed to Sophie.

"Did you ever notice how much Sophie is like Lotta?" he inquired irrelevantly. "Except for the hair, of course."

"Yes," said Stephen. "I had noticed it. That's another reason."

"You think Aunt Lotta would upset me?" Sophie asked her father, curiously, "Oh, no, father. I don't think that. I think—I think she might understand me."

"Let her come, Stephen," urged the doctor, patting Sophie's hand. "She has a right to come back. It will do you good to be upset, damn it. People get too confounded smug. Nothing's going to influence our Sophie here anyway. She can't think of anyone but Lynn, can you, Sophie?"

"No," said Sophie.

The doctor drew a letter from his inside pocket and tossed it on the marble-topped table.

"Jerome says he'll be back for the Fair," he announced. "Doesn't mention his wife, as usual. I suspect he's packed her off to Italy—the lakes—with a few thousand dollars. I don't know why he married her, though I've heard she's very beautiful."

"You've never seen her?" Sophie managed to ask. She tried to take her eyes away from the letter that symbolized him on the marble table.

"Never," the doctor assured them. "It looks to me like an ideal marriage. She's abroad or in New York most of the time and the two or three months she's in Washington, Jerome spends here. Now, could anything be more convenient? Fond of each other, too, I think, in their way. So Lotta told me, when I was in Washington last year. Lotta has met Lucile."

"About Lotta . . ." pursued Stephen, his massive face furrowed in thought. "She's sure to start talk or trouble of some sort, you know. Still you think she ought to come?"

"My dear Stephen," mocked the older man, "Lotta is a woman who must do exactly what she must do. It's ridiculous for us to discuss whether she's wise or prudent since there's nothing on God's green earth we can do to stop her. Look at Sophie, here. Do you suppose for one minute you could keep her from marrying Lynn—if you took it in your head it was a bad move? Of course not. And there you are. Sophie and Lotta are as like as two peas. I know. I'm in love with 'em both, by George. . . . By the way, Stephen, have you seen Velvet? Fred's

just taking her out, now . . ." he jerked his thumb in the direction of the meadow. "Three ribbons last year. She'll win more
this year. Look at her, now!"

Stephen followed the doctor to the window and pushing the
curtains aside the two men stood watching the stable favorite put
through her paces. Sophie sat with her hands folded still in her
lap, staring at the letter from Jerome lying on the table. Big, bold
handwriting—she could not look away. It sent out waves that
beat against her stomach. She trembled. It lay there—only a white
piece of paper but it carried him, it pulsed with his dark bewitch-
ment and drove panic through her veins. The room vibrated,
swung in the air, lost its damp funereal odor and breathed, flamed
with blood-red curtains and grinning rows of red books. Sophie
closed her eyes to relieve the intolerable excitement but a white
square danced before her shut eyes, a white square with black
handwriting. She lost all sense of time and place, knew only that
her body implored the torment of his presence.

"And if I never see him again," she thought, "this will go on
forever. . . . Perhaps he will never come back to Ashton. . . . After
all, remember the years when I never saw him. . . ."

She looked past the two men silhouetted against the window
and saw the splotch of green that was meadow, the blocks of red
that were stables and sheds. Round and round the green galloped
a black horse, sleek and beautiful. . . . Sophie looked quickly
away, remembering. . . .

The doctor turned back, smiling. He hesitated between the
sofa and a severe horsehair chair, suddenly whirled about and
flung up his hands.

"My God, I can't stand this room!" he cried. "That Della is a
fiend. She keeps it just the way Hattie kept it—God, you can
smell the narcissus from her coffin!—and then gets me trapped
in here to remind me of my infidelities! God, Stephen, women
are devils! Let's get out of here."

He rushed out of the room, his bewildered friend at his heels.

Sophie got up. She walked, hypnotized, to the table and touched the letter, traced with her forefinger the outline of his writing. If only she dared put it to her cheek—or to her throat . . . She went slowly into the hall, just as a little old woman, the Gardiner's ancient housekeeper, scurried into the parlor with a broom and dust cloth to repair whatever damages the callers may have caused. Della always kept the room exactly as Mis' Hattie had kept it. (There was a sweet lady, God rest her!)

Della drew the shades.

For days the roads were alive with spring wagons taking prize vegetables, preserves, piles of prayerfully-wrapped embroidery and drawnwork to the Fair Grounds at Center City. There were wagons with sleek stolid Jerseys peering from trellised cages, crates of exquisite white Manorckas, ruffled Buff Cochons, comfortably bourgeois Plymouth Rocks, squawking their desperation to the heavens, silly black ducks and richly-feathered white geese, and proud brutish rams and steers and enormous sows still bewildered by their recent scrubbing.

Every farm had its boast to make from the Angora cat of the Anderson sisters to the amazing jar of strawberry and prune conserve offered by the queer old hermit from the south Ridge. Families squabbled over which day they would visit the Fair, and in their bedrooms farm girls breathlessly devised costumes and dreamed of a romantic stranger. The wealthy, among these Mrs. Tom Hamilton, serenely engaged a suite at the Center City Hotel for the whole week, and lest she be lonesome Mrs. Hamilton had invited Anna Stacey to sleep on the couch of the starved-looking parlor—(leather couch, two straight chairs, quartered oak center table, copy of the *Family Journal,* November, 1896).

Anna had never gone back to Steubenville though her mother wrote that there were new boarders and it was hard work taking care of the place now that Clara had beaux all the time. Anna gritted her teeth and swore that she would never go back to make beds for young men who flirted with the lady boarders, and wash dishes in the steamy, garlic-scented kitchen while her younger sister giggled with her beaux on the front porch. She had been cheated here of Lynn Hamilton, it was true, but at least there was George Truelove to tantalize and to despise because he was so stupid as to worship herself. She hated Lynn, but at the same time she respected him for his indifference. Anna wrote to her mother that she was through being a slave. Let Clara work. As for herself, she expected to be married very soon to a rich man. p.s. Clara needn't think she could come and live with her when she got married.

Every morning Anna and Dora went down to the Fair Grounds, Dora tremendous in a brown taffeta suit with a trailing ruffled hem and a plumed hat tilted stylishly over her perspiring face, and Anna, hungry and beaten-looking, in a too-large faded pink linen suit and baby blue organdie hat set awkwardly above an inch of singed brown bangs. It elated Anna to seem a part of the festivity rather than a mere day visitor as the Coles, the Anderson girls, and the Trueloves were. She had even struck up a conversation with one of the men in the New Invention Pavilion—The Talking Machine, The Ice Cream Freezer—but then a frowsy blonde from the Woman's Exhibition spoiled that.

Buggies and wagons lined the streets of the self-satisfied little town, flags flew, bands played parading down the street, Civil War veterans marched, and a group of youngsters bore a Loyal Temperance Legion banner and sang "Saloons, Saloons, Saloons must go!" But on the contrary saloons had sprung up over night to meet the county's annual thirst. A fragrant alcoholic haze flung over the town, and tented the entire Fair Grounds. Streets were giddy with laughter and the shrill voices and megaphoned speeches of visiting politicians. There were clusters of starched white and flying ribbons here and there, groups of rosy farm girls giggling and ogling each passing man. By nighttime the groups— with good luck—would be scattered, each girl giggling with an awkward young man in some tree-shaded buggy behind the Fair Grounds, hysterically sipping from a jug of corn whiskey and abandoning herself to private yearnings. The wretched little frame hotels, supported comfortably all year by half a dozen traveling salesmen, now bulged with guests, and window shades were drawn night and day, boasting of the iniquity of their bedrooms. Carnival gods rode over the city and sprinkled the orthodox with their confetti.

The Trueloves' Bessie, on the plea of staying with the Coles' hired girl, stayed three days at the South Hotel with her barber and laughed herself sick over the spectacle of his scrawny little naked body. She ran with the Coles' hired girl in the daytime, for together they could make many new acquaintances. They wore red ribbons around their hair and red stockings and went arm in arm around the grounds, giggling and flirting and eating popcorn. The Coles' hired girl—her name was Tirzah—said, "Those fellows last night were married, did you know?" and then both clapped their hands over their mouths remembering what had happened.

"Well, *my* husband's never going to go to any Fair alone," said Bessie. "Not when I marry. Men are the limit!"

On the second day of the Fair, the Trueloves drove to Center City, George, Cecily and the three children in the spring wagon and Stephen and Grandmother Truelove in the phaeton.

Cecily asked Stephen over the old lady's head, "Don't you think it will be too hard on Mother to drive over to the Fair?

Supposing I stay home with her and let the rest of you go. There are so many things I must do before the wedding, anyway. I don't mind staying away this year."

"I tell you I'm not dead," quavered Grandmother, her eyes filling. "I haven't missed a Fair yet and I never felt better."

"But you're not eating well," admonished Cecily.

"Mother's all right," said Stephen. "Of course we'll go over."

"And the crowds upset her," persisted Cecily. "I really don't mind staying with her."

"I like crowds!" cried Grandmother. "I *always* like crowds. They do me good."

But when they arrived at the Fair Grounds and Stephen offered to help her out of the phaeton, she drew back her lace-mittened hand.

"I—if you don't mind, Stephen, I'll just sit here," she said. "I can see everything perfectly. You go and find the others."

"I'll come back and see how you are in a little while," Stephen smiled at her.

Grandmother Truelove sat rigidly in the phaeton, her head in its black-veiled bonnet held erect. The roan nibbled the leaves and impatiently switched its tail. Carriages and chattering people swarmed past into the wide-arched gateway. Grandma grew dizzy watching them. They ran, they shouted, they danced. They never stopped. There were pests crawling over her numb old body, and she was too tired to brush them off. There was something monstrous in their cruel vitality. She could not bear to watch them, and never, never could she mingle with them, even holding tight to her own Stephen's arm. She closed her eyes. The grotesque spectacle was wiped out. Sounds vanished—became a far, far-off melody, a dim, sad humming, became the droning of a fly above her bonnet. . . . She was old. She was old as Time. Presently she would die, be part of an ancient silence. She would be still. How cool and quiet a grave must be!

When Stephen came back she was asleep.

On the Fair Grounds the bands blared, strolling groups stopped to hail other groups, girls snickered and whispered, men guffawed or made grave wagers in quiet corners. In a pavilion a group of small boys in brass-buttoned uniforms—it was a city newsboys' band—made brave music, and here hanging over the rail early in the day Vera and Lois Winton were seen. Lois was exchanging demure smiles with a fat little boy who played the snare drum while Vera shouted taunts and boasts to a thin, narrow-faced young cornetist whose eyes were as rapacious as her own, and who appeared to have as scrupulous a respect for truth as Vera did. Later in the day Mrs. Truelove and Mary Cecily made a harassed search for the two children, aided by a loudly tearful Custer who sobbed of popcorn being torn from him, of lollypops snatched from under his nose, of wanton boxing of ears, and of two demon sisters who had torn a destructive trail through exhibits and pleasure pavilions in company with two equally vicious band boys.

Mrs. Truelove finally came upon the four engaged in a division of peanuts and lemon soda near the racetracks. Their ruffles were wilted, their hair ribbons, lost, their hair tangled about their hot, dirty faces.

"Children, we must be starting home," said Cecily patiently.

"Lookit!" said the thin-faced boy. He shoved a scarred red wrist under Mrs. Truelove's nose. "See? She bit me."

Vera remained calm.

"She's a very cruel girl, Aunt Cecily," said Lois sweetly. "She bit him till it bled. Do you think that's very nice?"

"Why did she do that?" asked Cecily.

"Because I wanted to," explained Vera and finished the lemon pop.

Cecily, in a burst of nervous force, seized one girl by each hand and made for the carryall. Custer bellowed along behind, wiping his eyes on his white linen sailor sleeve from which a red chevron drearily dangled.

"Paul is going to write a letter to me," said Lois, skipping along. "I have a beau now. But Vera bit Lewey so he's not a beau. He hit her with a stone."

"But it didn't bleed," boasted Vera. "I bit him till it hurt. I don't care."

"He hollered," said Lois.

"Catch me hollering," said Vera.

"You're naughty children," despaired Cecily. "I'm sure I don't know what your mother will say. What will you do when she gets here, I wonder!"

"Vera did take my lollypop," Custer woefully reminded her. "I'm going to tell."

"No, I am," insisted Lois. "I'm the oldest. I'm the one to tell Mama."

And then they were settled by Cousin Tom in the back of the carryall, their protests momentarily hushed by three sticks of striped peppermint.

Sophie and Lynn were staying over for the evening's dancing. They strolled about together, Lynn proud of his lady's perfection, the marvel of her still white hand on his arm, the warm ivory throat above the lace-frilled tight bodice, her proud red mouth and stormy dark eyes, the way her nostrils dilated, the shadow of her blue-black hair, against the brim of her leghorn hat. She was lovely, he thought, and she was his. Girls smiled at him and flung challenges, but he did not smile. His bride was on his arm and there was no other woman in the world nor would there ever be.

They wandered to the spot where the midafternoon crowd had gathered. Sophie exchanged greetings with Dora Hamilton, a little bewildered by the evident hatred in the eyes of the gray little person at Dora's side. Why did Anna Stacey look at her with such savage dislike? Dora, feeling Anna's clutch on her arm tighten at Lynn's approach, knew why Anna disliked Sophie, and was sorry for the poor ugly girl who would never in her life have a man to care for her. Lynn hardly saw Anna, his proud smile was for the whole world.

They moved on. The gaiety had brought color to Sophie's cheeks. The blend of music, shrill shouts, the strident discords of the carousel fed in her a hunger for vulgarity, though to herself she said, "This is not for me but for people like Bessie. This is cheap."

But still her eyes shone and her breath came a little faster. Standing near a pavilion was a tall man with heavy drooping shoulders and a bearing and dress foreign to the farming men. Sophie caught the dark familiar profile and drew a long breath. Inexplicably fury tore at her bosom when she saw laughing up at him a beautifully-groomed woman in a plumed black hat. Who was she? What was she to him? Certainly she belonged to another world than this, and as certainly she smiled as though she were in love with him.

"Senator Anderson's wife over there with Jerome Gardiner," Lynn said casually. "She's taking the Senator's place as judge in some of the contests. Handsome woman."

Sophie said nothing. She dared not look again, so appalled was she at this red rage that consumed her, as if that man were hers, as if there were a covenant between them. . . . Who was the man beside her, then, this husband-to-be, when the only man who possessed her was Gardiner? Later Sophie heard Lynn speaking to Gardiner before she was conscious of his approach. She looked up and saw his hat still raised waiting for her recognition. He had smiled at Lynn but there was a subtle entreaty in the glance he gave Sophie. Long after he and the handsome Mrs. Anderson had passed on, Sophie could not think of what words Lynn was saying to her, because of the blood pounding in her temples.

They met friends, people they saw only once a year at this very meeting place, people they saw every market day at the Ridge or at the Center. There were sly congratulations. But Sophie clung to Lynn's arm and was silent, knowing only that somewhere near was Jerome Gardiner. She saw him again as they came to a mob applauding prize awards in the prettiest girl contest. On the platform stood the winner, a rosy country girl with curly hair. Gardiner, as the most prominent of the judges, was presenting her with the roses that had that morning won the ribbon in the flower show. As the crowd shouted its approbation, old Doc Gardiner shouldered his way up to Lynn and Sophie.

"See here!" he boomed, clasping Sophie's hands. "Those roses belong here, eh Lynn?"

"Sophie doesn't have to go up on any platform," answered Lynn proudly. "Everyone knows she's the prettiest woman in this county."

The old man laughed. He nodded toward the platform.

"I told Jerome when he went into the judge's box that there was no use in giving a prize if Sophie Truelove wouldn't go into the contest. He said; 'I know it, Dad. I've seen Sophie Truelove.'"

Sophie looked away, but for the first time she was proud of her beauty, proud that he should have recognized it.

"Yes sir," boasted the doctor, twirling the ends of his white mustache, "My son has seen beauties the world over—Paris, Vienna, Rome—but he can't deny that your Sophie is the queen of them all, Lynn, my boy."

"I don't need to travel to know that, Doc," drawled Lynn.

"But I don't envy you your job, young man," declared the doctor, waggling a solemn forefinger. "As queens go, Sophie's a good girl, but they breed danger, my boy—these queens. Look out!"

Lynn laughed lazily, but Sophie was vaguely angered by the old man's mockery.

"I was afraid at first, Sophie," Lynn said, looking down at her after the old man had pushed on. "Remember? I swear I was afraid to see you again after that day in front of the post office. I said to myself, 'Steady, now. There's no happiness in a woman like that.' That's the reason I tried to stay away right afterward. I guess you never knew that."

"But you came back," Sophie said.

"I had to," was Lynn's laconic reply.

Lynn was simple and clear. In her mind Sophie rushed to him gratefully for a rest from her own questionings. And then they were caught again in the crowd and propelled slowly toward the outer gates. It was dusk and the carriages were leaving. Lights flowered over the Fair Grounds, and in the dancing pavilion the orchestra tuned up. Sophie and Lynn saw the Trueloves leaving for home with Custer squealing his disappointment from the backseat of the carryall. They saw the doctor drive by in his mud-spattered buggy, his linen duster fluttering out at the sides. Sophie wondered about Jerome and the Senator's wife from Washington. They had gone, too, perhaps. But even as she wondered she saw him coming toward her. He carried a huge basket of red roses in his arms. She wanted to look away, to show surprise that he should come back to her. But once their eyes had met there was no breaking the spell.

"We have seen each other only twice," she reminded herself. "There have been no words that could mean anything between us. This feeling—it does not exist. It does not," but the blood whirled again in her temples.

"Roses," said Jerome Gardiner, "must go where they belong. Will you take them, Miss Sophie?"

Sophie took the basket but she could not speak. She heard Lynn thanking him and was grateful but she could only bow her head. She followed Lynn to the buggy and the flowers splashed over the sides and over the dashboard. Lynn was proud of her, proud she was so fair that a great man like Jerome Gardiner should compliment her. He rebuked her gently for being so cold in her thanks.

But when later that night in the pavilion Lynn stood on the balcony watching Sophie dance with Gardiner, he wondered why they never spoke one word as they danced. The music stopped and began again but dance after dance went by and still those two danced silently round and round, the man on the balcony forgotten. Sophie had no sense of anything but Jerome's arm about her, the warmth of his body, the exciting heat of his breath. Once, in a shadowed corner, she knew his lips touched her hair.

Their feet moved in marvelous accord. They were part of the music, part of each other. . . . Suddenly Sophie sensed a pair of puzzled blue eyes upon her. She looked up at the balcony, and at once the lovely perishable thing vanished and she fell through space and stars to the moment. She abruptly dropped Jerome's arm and went to Lynn.

"Take me home, Lynn," she said.

"Tired?" Lynn forgot his momentary jealousy and smiled at Gardiner with the air of the accepted victor, one who could afford to be generous. Sophie drooped behind him, her face white and her black lashes strangely wet against her cheek. For an instant her hand lay in Jerome's; she gave him a dazed fleeting smile.

Even when she sat in the buggy going home, she thought of that other man. The horse jogged down the dark quiet road, and Lynn's arm encircled Sophie and her roses. Sometimes he bent and kissed her smooth cheek, sometimes he whispered, "Sophie . . ." and then stopped, for it seemed to him that he had said everything. But Sophie was back in the pavilion in Jerome Gardiner's arms, and their eyes were lost in each other's while their feet moved to a slow compelling waltz, and between them was a certain knowledge.

The horse jogged dreamily down the dark narrow road. Sophie bent over her flowers. The red roses were white in the starlight.

The farmhouse was alive long before daylight on the day of the Truelove Reunion and Sophie's wedding. Trains must be met at Center City, at Ashton Ridge, and at Ashton Center. All morning someone must be on hand to help unhitch the visitor's teams. Grandma Truelove had been up and dressed since three o'clock. She had peered out the window. No one else up. Not even John. A pretty how-de-do with people expected any minute. A pretty how-de-do. But that was like Cecily Mills. She didn't care about the Trueloves. Never had. She'd just as soon insult them as not. Supposing Walter from San Francisco—not back for forty years—should drive in. Nobody up to welcome him. Nobody after forty years. No hot coffee on the stove . . . Supposing Ellen and Arch from the East should come now, drive in the yard out there. Nobody up to say good-day to them. A pretty how-de-do. Supposing Lotta . . .

Grandmother Truelove sat twisting her gnarled hands restlessly. She limped over to the highboy and lit the lamp. She waited. In the henyard a cock soon to be executed crowed marvelously. The old woman could endure it no longer. She hobbled out into the dark hallway and stopped uncertainly before her son's door. She'd a good mind to rap on the door with her cane and tell Cecily it was high time someone went downstairs. . . . Well, at least she would wake Sophie.

She turned the knob of Sophie's door. It startled her a little by swinging open. In the dark room she could see a shadow against the window.

"Sophie—Sophie, are you up?" she demanded.

"Yes," came from her granddaughter in a choked voice.

Grandmother Truelove thrust her head forward and blinked in an effort to discern Sophie's face. She remembered that there was going to be a wedding today, too. She was a little foggy about the principals in the affair.

"Lotta's coming," she said simply.

Sophie made a little sound of assent.

The old woman felt relieved now that Sophie was up. Everything would be taken care of. Everyone would be welcomed. Sophie was ready for them. Sophie was her own self only warm and young and swift. She could go back and lie down—not to sleep, mind you—just to rest her back a little. Bones got tired. She pattered back to the door and then stopped.

"Somebody's going to be married today," she announced perplexedly. "Is it—is it Bessie? Bessie and John?"

Her granddaughter gave a little laugh.

"No, Grandmother," she said. "It's my wedding."

Grandmother Truelove felt suddenly weak. She found her way dizzily back to her room and climbed into her feather bed. Sophie. Sophie. And then a pleasant excitement stirred her. She was going to be married. She was twenty-one. She was going to marry Nathan Truelove. She was going to wear her white satin with roses brocaded on the train. She must get up and look at her veil again. Try it on in the candlelight. She must get up and look in the mirror to see if she looked any different on her wedding-day. Haughty black eyes, sleek black hair drawn over her small, perfect head, white petal-soft skin. Nathan said she was beautiful, but most people called her handsome. Nathan was a silent man. In another day his silence would belong to her. She must get up, get up and look in the mirror. . . .

And Grandmother Truelove fell asleep. When she awoke the Pecks from Indianapolis—her own sister's children—had been brought from the morning train and were shouting boisterously over breakfast in the dining room.

Mary Cecily and little Robert had arrived—they were going to stay a few weeks—and Cousin Caroline's family were climbing out of the carryall at the side door, laden with baskets of veal loaf, potato salad, and incredible cakes with icing an inch thick. George was out beyond the orchard putting the finishing nails in the long rustic tables and benches where the Reunion feast was to be held. Cecily scurried about the house, a bright flush on her thin cheeks, torn between her duties as hostess and her desire to hover over the daughter about to be a bride.

Mary Cecily was really supervising the wedding preparations. She had seen to it that the wedding gown was spread out in formidable magnificence over the four-poster bed in Sophie's room, with Grandmother Truelove's own yellowed veil folded beside it. The white slippers here with the stockings beside them. The blue garters. The four lace-frilled petticoats on the chair with a starched chemise. The lace-ruffled drawers. The new corsets. The prayerbook.

Sophie was pale and confused. She wanted it to be all over. She wanted Lynn to come and take her away. If she had no strength of her own then she must stay always where strength was. She despised herself. That all last night she should have crouched by the window holding out her arms for a stranger who must now be forever forgotten. She looked at the white satin gown laid stiffly out on the bed, its folds rigidly correct, a garment not for surrender, rather was it a suit of armor for a bride bewitched. The veil folded filmily beside it was for binding the bride's eyes, the white satin shoes were for staying her wayward feet, the ivory prayerbook for confounding evil memories. . . . Sophie dreamily fingered the white gown. In a little while this white hand would wear a wedding ring, surely a charm against dark spells . . . Ah, this was the hand Jerome Gardiner had kissed. . . .

All morning the aunts and uncles and cousins—fourth, fifth, even sixth, were arriving. They swarmed over the stable admiring the cattle and horses, over the fields admiring the corn, over the orchard admiring the Queen Annes, the red Astrakans, the russets. They talked of their cattle, their horses, their corn, their orchards, while on the porches the women talked of their babies and of coming confinements.

Vera and Lois found gullible cousins to whom they could boast of their Washington luxuries. In the parlor Custer was craftily examining the purple plush album to see if all the people had escaped from the album. It was that very night that he dreamed the uncles had all got out of the album and he had to catch them with aunts to match and lock them back in with the little gold key.

On the front piazza Grandmother Truelove sat wrapped in her Paisley against treacherous late summer winds, and graciously welcomed the cousins and nieces and all their children. She held their babies though she had long ago lost all interest in such usual things as babies and death, she squeezed the tiny hands and said to Caroline, whose youngest she held, that it really seemed to her that babies weren't so pretty as they used to be, and that mothers didn't dress them as prettily. Now Stephen and her boys always had their hand-embroidered dresses and bibs with crocheted medallions and edgings that took months to work. And Lotta—but where was Lotta? (Here, take this child!) Where was Lotta? Stephen said she was going to come today. Cecily said she was going to come. No, Cecily had said she might not come. But she would. Lotta would come.

But Lotta had not arrived by two o'clock when the two or three hundred guests sat down to their banquet. The Hamiltons were there, Lynn's father and Dora and some young cousins from downstate, because from now on the Hamiltons would be a part of Truelove Reunions as the Mills were and the Pecks. Each year there were more Mills and fewer Trueloves. In another decade perhaps it would be the Mills Reunion and the Trueloves would be only a small proportion just as a generation before it had been the Peck-Truelove Reunion until the Trueloves had so outnumbered the Pecks.

Grandmother Truelove in black bombazine sat at the head of the table and picked at a morsel of chicken loaf, smiling down at all her family, and wanting only Lotta. Her baby. But Lotta did not come. Grandma avoided Cecily's eye because she could read the triumphant gleam of relief there. Cecily didn't want Lotta. Cecily was spiteful. Cecily was a Mills.

Sophie sat beside Mary Cecily and looked over the long chain of faces noting curiously a family mark caricatured here, glorified there. One Adam Trygloe centuries ago had had wide-apart slanting eyes, a straight Greek nose and big perfect teeth, and here were babies with the barest perceptible traces of these characteristics, old men and women whose flesh had shrunken until they were not persons but the family symbol—slanting eyes, Greek nose, fangs of gleaming ivory. These totems were seated at evenly spaced intervals like key letters in a puzzle. A rosy, plump, young girl here seemed unique, an individual, and then placed between two of these tribal symbols revealed a fugitive but unmistakable resemblance to them—a gesture that belonged to women with slanting eyes, a flashing smile that was meant for flawless teeth. There were curious slants inside, too, Truelove ways of looking at life . . . Yet no two here could speak each other's language.

In her demurely curtained bedroom Sophie was being laced into her wedding gown. Her mother and Mary Cecily and the blonde cousin from St. Louis fluttered about her with powder and pins. Lois and Vera in amazingly starched white ruffles and pink bows were allowed to watch providing they sat very still.

Lois thought, "I will have white silk stockings when I get married, too, and my hair will be black and come to my knees."

Vera, on the edge of Lois's chair, thought, "In a little while Mama will be here and everyone—Bessie, too, and Miss Stacey—will see how pretty our mother is. I hope she has plumes on her hat and I hope she kisses me first."

"Well, children . . ." Cecily's mouth was full of pins—"so your mother didn't come after all!"

"She'll come," said Vera. Her mother had a box with scented lotions and pastes and delicious bouquets of false curls. Perfume in silver bottles.

Through the open windows poured the chatter and shrill gaiety of the guests. They were scattered over the orchard, around the disarranged banquet table, over the porches and the garden. Downstairs in the parlor Stephen and Bessie were putting anxious last touches to the flower-massed archway, fussing over the rows of chairs, conferring with the minister from Center City.

"We'll get the setting sun this way," said Stephen.

"Is that a good omen?" discreetly inquired the minister.

Sophie was curiously hushed in the midst of all the confusion. Her brocade fell in sculptured folds from her waist, and her mirror showed scarcely a line where the ivory of her throat modulated into the ivory of the gown. She knew that never had she looked more lovely.

"He would not forget me if he saw me now," she thought, and then was shocked at her own infidelity. That she could think of another man at her wedding! She remembered Lynn across the hall with Hart Purvis, his best man. It was Lynn she truly loved. And in another hour she would be his forever, safe from strange heavy eyes, safe from shadowy monstrous dreams. Safe forever. Sophie crumpled abruptly on Cecily Truelove's tense shoulder.

"Mother . . ." she sobbed.

"Why, Sophie!" exclaimed Cecily nervously. "Now, now, Sophie! You'll get yourself all mussed. There, there now. Don't be frightened. It's something all of us must go through!"

Sophie silently dabbed at her eyes with the lace square. But she knew Aunt Lotta, if she were here, would understand that sudden terror. Aunt Lotta would know it was terror only of oneself, of the hidden things that were in one to do . . . Sophie smiled at her mother to show how completely she was in command of herself. She wanted Lotta—but Aunt Lotta did not come.

Much later when John was proudly driving the bridal pair to the train, the Truelove carriage gave way on the Center Road to a hired carriage from Center City. Sophie, in that moment, caught a glimpse of a pale blonde woman in a black-plumed hat, whose slanting eyes met Sophie's with curious recognition.

"Aunt Lotta!" exclaimed Sophie, but the carriage had gone on, and in its wake the dust was flung into fantastic ghostly shapes.

Sophie turned her face to her husband.

It was a dream, Lotta thought, that she was again moving through dusty weeds stooping under low branches of apple trees toward that spreading farmhouse. How heavy her feet were now, she marveled, and how light they had been when in flight, they last touched this grass! Truelove faces all about—cousins, aunts, uncles—but these faces were no more real than goblin faces she had seen. Here were her children—she bent and kissed them—and Stephen, holding her hand with pathetic tenderness. Stephen had changed. Everyone had grown old and different. Only the secret wonder in their eyes when they looked at her remained the same, and now there was more curiosity than ever in their glances. But Lotta, her eyes shadowed with old suffering, stayed beside her children, and no one questioned her about the things they yearned to know, for they were still afraid of her.

Miraculously, then, the Trueloves and the Mills and the Pecks had driven off and trains whistled far away reminding the empty, overturned tables in the orchard of two who had sat here or there, and that now one had gone East, one West, and the three hundred children of one Adam Trygloe had scattered once again over the continent.

Grandmother Truelove sat by the window in the dusk of the early moon, and her old eyes were fixed on the driveway.

"Lotta's gone," she whimpered.

Stephen shook his head at Ephraim a little gravely.

"No, Lotta's here," said Cecily. (She dared not talk to her! She dared not show her fear!) "Lotta's waiting for you to speak to her. It's Sophie who went away."

"Lotta's gone," repeated the old woman. "My poor little Lotta."

In the corner Lotta sat twisting the rings on her slender fingers and wondering what had driven her back to this house. She had had to come, that she knew, but why? Upstairs her three children slept. . . . They had never needed her. (Vera was dreaming of herself as a tall beautiful bride and her mother weeping, "I never understood you, Vera. Forgive me, my darling favorite child.")

"Mother has counted on your coming for years," Stephen whispered to his sister. "What a pity she's so confused now that you're really here."

"She's nearly eighty-seven," said Cecily.

"Lotta's gone away," mourned the old woman vacantly. "My baby Lotta."

Lotta closed her eyes and in a moment of dim ecstasy saw Death in the air. She leaned her yellow-haloed head against the wall and remembered things. She could see herself, a girl in a white dress running through the orchard at night—she was going to him! she was going to him!—could feel again the perfume of clover and familiar blossoms grown strange and luring at night, could see far off that lace of young fir trees against the moon. His carriage was waiting for her down the road, but long before she reached it she knew she was not alone, that fleeing with her, their moonlit draperies in the wind, their hair blowing, their feet never touching earth, were others, pale, lovely women running—running—to a lover waiting at the turn in the road. In their wide eyes as they smiled at her there was no wisdom, only an eagerness for pain. . . . Why had she returned? Then she thought of that moment today when her carriage flew past the bridal carriage and a face startlingly like her own had peered out at her. It was for this one she had come back—for Sophie. But now she was too late. . . .

Lotta got up and went over to her mother's chair.

"Mother," she said gently. But the old woman only stared at her with vacant unhappy eyes.

"Lotta's gone," she mourned. "My baby's gone away."

Long after the family had gone to bed, Stephen Truelove stood in the doorway of the kitchen drinking in the warm tranquillity of the summer night. His little Sophie was gone, and now that she had fled he could recall only the exquisite little girl who had sat

beside him in the carriage going to market, the little ivory figurine who sat in sculptured silence while awed farmers and rosy
wives pointed at her.

They had confided little in each other, he and Sophie. They
were that kind. But they had understood each other's silences, as
he and Lotta had theirs. Now she was gone.

Stephen sighed.

Behind him he heard a faint stir and then Lotta brushed lightly
past him. A filmy shawl was thrown over her shoulders, and
above it her face looked incredibly like Sophie's. The confused
mass of her hair was caught up in a loose knot in which a rhine-
stone comb gleamed. She said no word but hurried across the
grass toward the orchard. Stephen saw her disappear among the
trees and was impelled to follow her. . . . He cast a guilty glance up
to the room where Cecily lay sleeping. Cecily never liked queer
things—walks in moonlight, awe over sunsets, moods over organ
music. She would blame Lotta for this. . . . He was already in
the moonlight-patterned shadow of the orchard, and Lotta
had turned.

"Why did you follow?" she asked him.

"I wanted to talk to you," Stephen answered. "To tell you . . .
to ask you . . ."

"Poor Stephen," Lotta said softly.

"You think Sophie will not be happy—then?" Stephen demanded.

"I am afraid," Lotta answered. "Sophie is our blood, Stephen,
and we attract suffering."

"But they love each other," Stephen said. "There's never been
anyone else with Sophie."

"Sophie is our blood," repeated Lotta. "She will suffer as you
did over Kate. . . ."

"You—you understood all that?"

Lotta nodded.

"When they told you Kate Maxwell was dead, you turned as white as that moon. I knew then."

Stephen was silent. Now he had forgotten Sophie and thought of his own years of unhappiness.

"A man should be able to forget," he mused. "Sometimes I wonder if . . . but of course I could never have left Cecily. Even if there hadn't been the children."

"Poor Stephen," Lotta said. "Of course you couldn't. Women do the foolish things. If you had been a woman nothing would have held you. But a man . . . even when you knew your happiness lay with Kate you just couldn't go to her. Men are like that."

"But after all, Lotta, why should I be so sure that she could have given me happiness," answered Stephen. "There might have been others—after me. I would have gone through hell."

"It's nonsense to talk of this now," he went on, while Lotta stroked the bark of the tree, her eyes far down the roadway. "After all she's dead. Dead twenty years and more. But I can't keep from thinking of her. You know, Lotta, just as if she were here. As if she was my wife. It hurts that she died the way she did, with me forgotten . . . as if that week meant nothing."

"You're so sure she forgot?" Lotta asked him.

Stephen gripped her hand.

"You know things like that, Lotta—things about dead people—tell me."

Lotta was silent. When she finally spoke her voice seemed far away.

"She never forgot, Stephen," she said. "Never in all this world or the next. She would come to you after all these years if she were alive, though you would never ask that. Kate never forgot you. Perhaps she did write to you."

"No," said Stephen. He wanted to know, but Lotta's queer fixed smile struck him with unaccountable terror.

"You don't know," she said, "letters can be destroyed."

Now the trees about her seemed alive, their branches waving slowly, slowly, though there was no wind. Stephen found himself breathing heavily, staring at this woman leaning against the tree, this creature who had been his own sister.

"Shall we go in?" he panted.

Lotta shook her head, still smiling faintly.

"Good-night, Stephen," she said. "Go back to Cecily again. Tell her that a dead woman has held out her arms to you. Good-night, Stephen."

He could not speak, and he knew that his hands were shaking curiously. He should not go in now, and leave her, but he dared not take her arm—and this thing she had momentarily become did not belong in houses. . . . She had told him what he had wanted to know, but he could not bear knowing. He lay in bed for hours shuddering with the weight of icy arms about his neck, with stiff frozen lips scourging his face with kisses.

School began with a very fat solemn little boy in blue overalls emerging from a shabby farmhouse way down the Ridge road and trudging along in the dust with a slate under one arm and a lunch pail dangling from the crook of his elbow. At the corner of the Ashton Center turn this small person stood still, yanked the lid from his pail, removed the apple and ate it. As the last bite—seeds, worms and all—was consumed, a gawky, red-haired girl in green-checked gingham long outgrown appeared on the Center Road leading a screaming little boy by the hand. This was Sister and Baby Greer. The three took up the road to-gether until the next turn where they stopped for Baby Greer to gobble the cookie from his lunch basket. Then three other children came scurrying down the side road, two of them loudly whooping and waving their slates. The third walked demurely behind, carrying stiffly before her a bouquet of four exhausted asters and an angry fern.

"I'm going to sit in a front seat," said Custer boldly to Baby Greer. "Miss Stacey said I could."

Baby Greer stuck out his tongue. Sister cuffed him. He bellowed.

"I'm going to walk over here if Baby's going to bawl," said Lois, daintily picking her way across the road. She had on a new hair ribbon, red, and new shoes that squeaked delightfully.

"Custer's a crybaby, too," said Sister.

"I am not," wept Custer.

"Will you shut up?" ominously demanded Vera.

Custer was silent. There were still marks on his cheek where Vera had scratched him. Custer respected Vera. Sister resumed hold of Baby's hand. Vera pranced behind her older sister imitating her mincing steps and holding out an imaginary bouquet.

"See . . ." she mocked, "I'm taking a bouquet to the Teacher."

Lois blushed indignantly and tossed her head.

"So'm I," giggled Custer, tears still undried on his face. "Lookit!"

He drew a small garter snake from his pocket. The little girls, excepting Vera, shrieked and ran, Sister's red pigtails standing out straight behind her in horror.

Vera glowered.

"Can't you keep a secret?" she demanded. "Give me back my snake. Now they'll tell."

The road was suddenly agitated by half a dozen more squealing children. The smallest Cole girls and their big brother ran from behind a hedged front lawn and added their squealing to the chorus. Baby Greer and Custer stopped to indulge in a round of scratching and kicking until pulled apart by their sisters. The school bell could be heard pealing, whereupon a dismal silence fell upon the group. With bowed heads they wandered up to the little square frame schoolhouse, just as a fat pony cart containing a prim, starched little girl—Letty Cross—drove up. Immediately the group was united.

"Baptist legs! Baptist legs! Baptist legs!" they shrieked, running after the pony. It stopped and the little girl got out, tearfully.

"Baptist legs!" they yelled, until the teacher appeared in the schoolhouse door and the little Cross girl walked haughtily up the path under the protection of Miss Stacey's cold eyes.

Anna Stacey went back to her desk. It had begun again. This morning when she had left the house, Lucy Anderson looked up from her morning cup of tea and said, "Never mind, dear, there's worse things than being a teacher, and as for being an old maid, Sara and I really enjoy our freedom, don't we, Sara?"

How they loved to twit her with her fate, how they adored seeing someone else suffer the humiliations they had suffered! So skilled in cruelty were they that they had guessed her feeling for Lynn Hamilton and never missed an opportunity at a sly jibe. Now that the fuss over her being the new teacher was all over, no one paid any attention to her. Newness had been her only charm for the swains of the countryside. Hart Purvis had taken her home from church twice and then started "going steady" with a girl in Center City. . . . There was that night she had smiled up at him in church and he walked right past her to the Center City girl, and she had walked home alone down the dark road, the taunting little smile still fixed on her lips.

George Truelove she hated. She hated him because he was Sophie's brother, and because he was stupid and because he was not Lynn Hamilton. No, she would grind him into mincemeat before she ever gave in to him! Let his sister see how one person despised the Trueloves! Let her see!

Sitting at her desk in her black voile dress, Anna bit her lip and lavished a special hate upon each pupil as he or she took a seat. ("Good-morning, Teacher." "Morning, Teacher." "Morning, M'Stacey.") She could have screamed. Pests. Plagues. She hated their shrill nasal voices, and the way they held their mouths open every time she spoke to them. She hoped they would be unruly so she could shake them. The three children from the Truelove farm stared at her with their slanting, shrewd eyes. She could read their malice, "You're back because you couldn't get a husband. You wanted Cousin Sophie's Lynn, but you can't have anyone Sophie wants." The last bell. Then the singing, "Flow gently, sweet Afton" . . . She would scream if she had to endure those high quavering voices day in and day out for another year. She took a piece of chalk and wrote savagely on the blackboard the day's lesson. Slate pencils scratched.

"You spelled believe wrong," said Vera Winton.

Miss Stacey rubbed out the word, heard the tittering behind her, hated them all. No, she would not stand it. She would not. . . . The wretched day dragged along. Spelling, reading, numbers, scrambling for lunch baskets, writing, singing. . . . The air was jabbed with reprimands and parabolas of tittering. The big Tompkins boy was impudent and was told to stay after school, but at four Anna Stacey saw him sneaking off before the others and she made no sign. She watched them sorting out their empty lunch pails and wanted to push them, to shoo them out the door. She hated them. She hated tomorrow. . . . "You spelled believe wrong," that child had said.

"I want you to stay, Vera Winton," she said on an impulse.

Vera about to follow the others, stopped, sulkily at the desk. The others were outside and a loud yell ascended the sky. There was a cry of "Baptist legs! Baptist legs!" when the unfortunate dissenter from the district's Congregationalism rode away in her pony cart. Vera looked regretfully out the window and then back at Anna Stacey.

"You're too impudent, Vera," Anna said quickly, embarrassed at having no more definite charge to bring. "I won't have it, I tell you."

Vera only looked at her with cold scorn.

"Don't you hear what I tell you?" the teacher was stung to cry out. "I won't have you looking like that. You Winton children are the worst children in the class."

"Oh no, we're not," Vera retorted, her eyes slanting contemptuously. "You know perfectly well we're not. You're just mad at us on account of Cousin Sophie. You're jealous, because she's engaged to Lynn Hamilton."

"Lynn Hamilton—pooh!" Anna felt her cheeks flaming and tried to subdue the quick anger in her voice. "The only person Sophie Truelove could ever get!"

"It's not so!" Vera flared. "Cousin Sophie could have any man in the world she wanted. Lynn . . . or Mr. Gardiner . . ."

Anna leaned across the desk. "Jerome Gardiner would never look at her!" she challenged. "A man like that is used to fine things. . . ."

"But he did look at her!" Vera answered triumphantly. "And I've seen him do it, too. Look, Cousin George's come to take us home!"

She bolted out the door just as a horse and highly polished buggy drew up at the hitching post. Anna Stacey looked after her with narrow eyes, saw Vera with Lois clambering into the buggy, Custer resolutely at their heels. Her lip curled at the sight of George making his way, rather self-consciously, through the crowds of children. . . . ("You're jealous because she's engaged to Lynn Hamilton. . . .")

George stood in the doorway, fumbling with his cap.

"I thought I might give you a lift home," he said. "I was just driving by from the Ridge."

"Out of your way, isn't it?" mocked Anna Stacey.

George reddened.

"No," he said. "I expected to drop by at my sister's."

"Your buggy's full," said Anna. "I'm afraid there's not room for any more."

George saw his three small cousins waiting alertly in the buggy, and the cords of his neck swelled.

"I'm not going home!" he called to them. "Get out!"

The three did not budge.

"We'll go for a ride," said Vera.

"No, you won't," roared George.

Anna demurely pinned on her black horsehair hat.

"You might as well take them," she advised him. "I'd rather walk ten miles than ride with you anyway."

George gasped. He wanted to protest but there was nothing to say. He backed out of the door while she placidly locked her desk and the windows, then picked up her pile of papers to be graded. He walked slowly down the path.

Anna Stacey twisted the key in the schoolhouse door.

"You're sure of that?" George turned and asked.

Anna smiled sweetly at him.

"Perfectly sure," she said.

George climbed into the buggy, pushing his three cousins with particular vehemence. He picked up the reins. Then he looked at the thin little woman in black with the white face who stood on the schoolhouse steps.

"Well—good-bye," he said.

"Good-bye," she said as they drove off.

She hated him. If there were no men on earth but Trueloves she would still hate him. But that was not saying she might not marry him.

George Truelove was the sort of man who believed that a slap from a girl indicated an interestingly passionate—though suitably discreet—nature. He had heard men in Clem's and the Ashton Center poolroom tell of their courting.

"... and when she cuffed me for trying to steal a kiss, I knew she was the girl for me. Yes sir, we've been married fifteen years."

"Well, does she still cuff you?"

"By ginger, she does!"

A woman, George and these men believed, was for a man's conquering, and there was little sport in following a girl who had no desire to run, who held out her arms for the pursuer. George himself burned with Anna Stacey's repeated insults, but never did he have any notion of giving up the chase. Even during the uncomfortable ride home from the schoolhouse, his purpose did not flag, though his ears remained purple with humiliation.

"I guess Miss Stacey don't like you much, Cousin George," said Vera.

"Custer, you must thank Cousin George for coming to drive us home," admonished Lois. "Say thank you to Cousin George."

"Aw, shut up," Custer urged her.

George cracked the whip and Lois forgot her disciplinary duties in the excitement of racing, though she did feel that Custer was naughty and rapidly getting out from her control. George paid small heed to his young cousins. He would call on her, George thought, some Saturday afternoon when the Anderson girls had gone to market. He would have it straight out with her. Maybe she didn't like him. All right. Let her say so. He'd know where he stood, and for that matter he'd heard men say that lots of times women fought right up to the minute of the proposal, and then said yes, meek as a lamb.

George waited a week, and then one Saturday afternoon he drove to Ashton Ridge. On the way home he walked his horse past the tangled, ragged-fenced fields where the Andersons' two cows and ancient Dobbin pastured. His chin was set firmly with the determination of a man charging into battle rather than one about to make a sentimental enterprise. At the hitching stone he got out and left his roan to reflect on the neat, aster-sprinkled ruins of Miss Lucy's flower garden. He went up the cobbled path to the house—a great square gray shell with vine-hidden windows behind which old maids for two generations had peeped out at romance. As he pulled the front doorbell, the air upon the moment seemed filled with the flutter of petticoats, the tap of high heels on stairs, the whisperings of spinsters agog. Then hush . . . a cough . . . Miss Lucy herself at the door in a coquettish pink chambray, a heavy green-veiled hat on her head.

"Oh—you're going out?" George asked hopefully. He had been almost positive that both Anderson women would be in town this afternoon.

"Dear no!" giggled Lucy. "I have on a hat because I always wear a hat. With the garden to take care of; you're just running in and out all the time so we keep our hats on. It saves bother, really."

Sure enough Sara appeared behind her sister, her withered face framed in a similar hat. Anna Stacey could have told him that the two old maids wore their hats to breakfast, and even on winter days sat by the fire from morning to evening without removing them. It was not the garden but an experiment in dyes many years ago that had made the Andersons sensitive about their bare heads. There were still strange purple and green streaks in Lucy's scanty locks, and a variety of cerise, lavender and chocolate shades in Sara's that gave her sister complete nausea in those brief moments in the bedroom when they revealed their mutual eccentricities. Out of deference to each other they wore their hats. Natty felt tricorns with kimonos as they pared their nails in their bedroom. Velvet poke bonnets with calico aprons as they made a two-egg angel cake in the kitchen. Venerable plumed Gainsboroughs as they milked the cows in the stable yard. Their storeroom was filled with hats for they had never thrown away any of their clothes from earliest girlhood.

When Anna Stacey had put her meager trunk in the storeroom, she had looked about at the trunks and racks full of musty gowns, and thought sardonically of the hopes each new gown had meant. And there they hung, rotting—hundreds of them. On the top of her own trunk lay her gray satin, the dress that was to have been irresistible to Lynn Hamilton. Beneath it was the white muslin that was to have intrigued Hart Purvis—there was something of Lynn about Hart Purvis, she always thought. Savagely Anna banged shut the trunk. She would not be like those old maids. She would not.

But perversely enough, since her prospects were so scarce she had fled out the back door to the spring house the instant George's buggy had stopped at the door. And now Lucy and Sara, amazed and envious of this indifference, were trying to explain to George that Anna had just stepped out to the barn to see if Dobbin's cold was any better. Wouldn't George step in and have a cup of tea?

Sara, not observing Lucy's warning eyebrow, pushed open the parlor door and revealed in the midst of that awful austerity—preserved funeral wreaths, dead ancestor's curls under glass, ashes of theosophic aunts, portraits after death of apoplectic uncles—two pairs of pink woolen drawers on a drying rack by the fireplace. It was the only place the spinsters dared hang these intimacies, since out in the yard or kitchen the fact that they were drawers would embarrass their hired man, who was always running in and out, and in their bedroom the fact that they were this passionate color would amuse Anna Stacey. The parlor, never being used, was completely safe, until Sara so impetuously had revealed its dreadful secret to George Truelove.

George, however, gave no sign at the revelation, and walked composedly on into the dining room. To him their pink drawers were no more ridiculous nor astonishing than their outer garments. He was embarrassed chiefly at his own situation—being left alone with these two absurd old women—when it was Anna Stacey he had come to see. He had steeled himself to deal with Anna, and here he must sit on the edge of a chair, one eye on the window, listening to Sara twitter while Lucy brewed tea. Suddenly he caught a glimpse of color out by the spring house. He leaped from his chair, and strode out through the kitchen past Lucy—she was holding her veil streamers back with one hand and dangling a tea ball in a steaming kettle with the other.

In the dark cool spring house Anna sat, among the crocks of unskimmed milk, stone jars of buttermilk, and loaves of fresh butter. She could see George coming down the back walk, and she shrugged her shoulders.

"Well," she said coldly when he opened the screen door.

"You knew I came to see you," he accused her.

"What if I did?" she taunted him. "I don't have to see you, do I? Nobody ever told me I had to see anyone I didn't want to."

George caught her by the wrists.

"Yes, you do," he said through his teeth—he was amazed at his own rage. "I came here to ask you to marry me, and by God you've got to answer.

Anna did not flinch, though his fingers were strong and hurt her thin wrists cruelly.

"Do I?" she jeered. "Well, I hate you, George Truelove. I hate you, do you hear? Despise you!

"I don't care," said George thickly. "You don't love anybody."

"I do," retorted Anna. "I love somebody and no matter if you and I were married for fifty years I'd leave you in a flash if I thought he wanted me. I'd poison you if he wanted me to. Oh yes, I love somebody all right."

George thought fleetingly of Hart Purvis, now engaged to the Center City girl, and he said triumphantly, "Well, he doesn't want you. What are you going to do about that?"

"I hate you, I said. Let go of my wrists!" cried Anna.

"I didn't ask you whether you hated me or not," said George grimly. "I asked you if you would marry me. Yes or no, now, be quick."

Anna saw Sara tiptoeing down the path to the spring house. She sprang to her feet.

"Yes," she spat at him, and started for the door just as Sara gently opened it.

"Oh!" exclaimed Sara. "Why I had no idea you were here, Anna. I wanted to tell George his horse is eating our asters."

George, victorious, saw his affianced slipping past Sara and running to the house. He felt baffled and strangely defeated.

"What? What?" he asked stupidly.

Sara leered at him.

"You naughty man!" she archly reproached. "You frightened our little Anna. Now run and tie your horse properly, and then you shall have a nice little cup of tea."

George blindly brushed her aside and went out. At the kitchen door he stopped an instant.

"Anna!" he called. "Anna!"

But there was no answer. When Lucy came to the door he mumbled some excuse, then went to his horse and drove away.

From an upstairs window Anna watched him, her eyes glittering.

Perhaps this was happiness, Sophie thought, with Lynn in their new home. Was it not what she had dreamed for so long, was it not what every woman should desire? But it troubled her that there should be so little of calm content in her happiness, so much of the fearful defiant joy of last moments. Lynn's adoration gave her no feeling of security in his absence. She dreaded to have him leave the house in the morning for it seemed to her that never had her loneliness been so intense, so shot with unrest. Perhaps this was love, Sophie thought, and in time it would give all her hours serenity, that other woman who fed on darkness and forbidden longings would be banished forever.

But over the sunlit breakfast table she could not speak sometimes, so desolate was she thinking that in another moment he would spring up, snatch his broad hat from the rack and be off to the fields or the stable with Will Carter. Only an hour ago she had lain locked in his arms, secure from all sensation but this, and now her flesh seemed still warm from contact with his body. She could not bear to have the spell broken and her loneliness restored to her. Sometimes, to put off their separation, she would get up from the table and walk with Lynn out the trellised path to the stable, her hand in his arm, their fingers interlacing.

Lynn was gravely proud of her dependence.

"Look, Sophie," he would say, waving his hand. "Our fields. Do you realize it, Sophie? Our house back there. Our cattle. Our granaries. Our home. Yours and mine."

And he would kiss her. Sophie's hand tightened in his clasp and she threw her head back. She was so strong, so free when she was with Lynn, as if a clear heavenly light shone through her. She didn't like to go back to the house. Even with the sunlight flooding her rooms, there were gray shadows where she dared not look, shadows that belonged to Sophie Truelove and not to Sophie Hamilton.

In her parlor was the old organ that had belonged to Lynn's mother, and above it hung two daguerreotypes. One, of Lynn's mother, a slender woman with splendid eyes and half-smiling lips. The other was of a little boy whose eyes looked fearlessly into Sophie's. That was Lynn at six. Sophie would take the picture in her hand and study it for a long time. If she had a little boy he would look like that, adorable with proud eyes and mouth. Even at six Sophie reflected she could have leaned on him, could have found security in his eyes. Perhaps that was why his mother half-smiled, knowing that her babe protected her with his small arms, that he was stronger than she.

One afternoon Sophie's mother came over with Vera, Lois and Custer having driven on to the Ridge store with George. Cecily fluttered from one end of the house to the other, examined the rag rugs in the bedrooms, the ruffled dimity curtains upstairs, the starched counterpane, the embroidery on the pillow shams, the china and glass wedding presents displayed in the china cabinet in the dining room, the mahogany of the downstairs rooms. Sophie would have no black walnut, and while maple or cherry was all very well for the bedrooms it must be mahogany in the downstairs rooms. Vera she left seated near Sophie's desk where she could refer discreetly from time to time to pigeonholes and secret drawers. Coming into the parlor Cecily threw up her hands.

"My dear child!" she exclaimed in horror. "Look at your shades! All the way up. The sun is simply pouring in here. And in the sitting room, too!"

Sophie shrugged.

"I don't like darkness, Mother," she said.

"I know," protested Cecily. "But the sun will ruin your furniture. It will fade the roses in your beautiful Brussels carpet. Now, Sophie!"

"Perhaps," said Sophie, "but while it shines it makes them seem so much brighter."

There was no arguing with Sophie, though it broke Cecily's heart to see such furniture sacrificed for a temperamental whim. She blamed herself for not being as rigorous as some housewives in teaching her children a reverence for furnishings as works of art. She must be more severe with Lotta's children, she thought. She thought of the perfect Anderson parlor, of the Gardiner parlor. . . .

"The Gardiner's Della says she hasn't let the sun in their parlor since Hattie died," Cecily said reproachfully. "Things are exactly in as good a condition as they were twenty or thirty years ago. Really, Sophie!"

"I don't want a parlor like the Gardiner's," Sophie said in a low voice. (That white letter on the marble-topped table!)

Cecily sighed.

"Well, for my part I'm sure it always seemed very fine. Of course they never had a great lot of children running through the house the way we've had. The doctor came in last night. He wanted to look at Vera's throat again. He asked about you. Said he was coming over some day while Jerome was here. He wanted Jerome to know the prettiest girl in Ohio. That's the way he put it."

"He mustn't come here!" Sophie cried in alarm.

Cecily looked surprised.

"Why, Sophie, I never thought you would be shy about callers. Goodness knows we've always had a deal of company, and you'll have to get used to it because Lynn's well-liked. I daresay the doctor will come alone anyway, because Jerome is sporting around with his horses all the time he's home."

Sophie drew a long breath.

"I wonder why Lynn doesn't come in," she said. "He's been gone all day. I do miss him so much."

"Lonesome?" Cecily patted her daughter on the shoulder. "There, there, my dear, I never expected you to be as silly as most brides. My goodness, we farmers' wives have to get used to being alone in the house all day. Nights, too. Lynn'll be driving to the city to see about lumber or machinery some of these days and then you'll be alone for sure. Unless you come over to the farm and stay."

"I'm not afraid of being alone," Sophie smiled. "Not in my own house."

Her mother bustled back to the sitting room in quest of her niece. George would be stopping for them any minute now, and he didn't like to be kept waiting. Vera must put her things on immediately. Vera was reading a bundle of congratulations letters found in the top desk drawer but so absorbed was she in their contents that she asked, "Who is Uncle Wallace?" before she remembered to be embarrassed.

"Uncle Wallaces are the Montana Trueloves," said Cecily. "They didn't get here this year for the Reunion because Aunt Bertha had a tumor. My, what a curious little body you are! Come, now, get your bonnet. I hear George out there now!"

Cecily fastened on her own bonnet and pushed Vera before her out the back door.

"Remember, Sophie," she urged. "You won't have any color in your rug if you let the sun shine on it. Keep the shutters closed. You'll ruin your house with sunlight."

Sophie only smiled. She waved to the children in the buggy outside with George.

"I'm not going to have any shutters on my house," said Vera. "What do you think of that, Cousin Sophie?"

"Probably a very good idea," answered Sophie.

"Hush!" rebuked Cecily. "It's not nice to talk that way. Come, Vera."

They drove away. Sophie went back into the parlor and almost feverishly took down the daguerreotype of Lynn. But the

direct grave eyes could not banish the memory of a white envelope throbbing on a marble-topped table. No, even the sunlight
could not reach every corner.

That night long after she was in bed something wakened
Sophie, something as sharp as the sound of a shot. She sat up in
bed rigidly, her black hair tumbling over her shoulders, one hand
clutching her throat. She could hear horse's hoofs galloping over
the Ridge road.

"What—what is that?" she choked.

Lynn drowsily lifted his head from the pillow.

"Nothing to be frightened of," he reassured her. "Probably
Gardiner out for a night ride. Go back to sleep, dear. He used to
ride over to Ashton Center and back every night when he was
home. Just a freak. Probably takes the Ridge road now because
it's in better shape. Nothing to be afraid of."

Sophie lay down, her heart still thundering as terrifically as
the horse's hoofs. Long after the sound had vanished she lay
wide-eyed, panic-stricken. After that she was wakened each
night by a penetrating sense of danger, and she would lie in
tense waiting for the horse to come galloping into sound. It was
always just a moment after her awakening. Then Sophie remained rigid—breathless—until it had galloped off into silence
again. Sometimes she was seized with an almost unconquerable
impulse to rush out the window and fly to meet that rider. Then
she would grip the side of the bed and clench her teeth until the
impulse had passed. By morning those moods seemed absurd
and inconceivable to her, after Lynn's arms had circled her and
her cheek had felt the warmth of his shoulder. But one midnight
Lynn wakened to find her standing by the open window, her
black hair swirling down, her eyes wide and staring in the
moonlight.

He sprang out of bed and took her hands in his, leading her
gently back. She lay in his arms sobbing like a child all night.

On the distant road a man galloping through the darkness thought of Sophie Truelove.

On Sundays Bessie put an extra leaf in the dining table for it was the day of the weekly family dinner. Sophie and Lynn came over, sometimes Tom and Dora Hamilton, and now George's fiancée came regularly, her mouth sulky, her eyes defiant. Bessie sat at the foot of the table, next to Mrs. Truelove and was perpetually jumping up to bring in enormous second helpings from the kitchen. It pleased her today to ignore John in her zealous generosity, to lift her eyebrows when he cleared his throat preliminary to a feeble request for stewed corn.

"What—more?" she would demand coldly.

"Damn it, I haven't had any yet," John would be driven to retort.

He sat between Vera and Lois, uncomfortable over the delight that his audible enjoyment of food gave to the children. Scrubbed, he looked boiled and slightly underdone, as if he had been served a little too soon. His color deepened under Bessie's malicious jibes and between bites his lips would move in imaginary repartee.

Grandma Truelove sat on Stephen's right and permitted a senile vagueness to come over her face whenever Cecily spoke to her.

"What was it Hannah just said?" she would ask gently of Stephen, as if; Cecily thought, she did not know her daughter-in-law's first name, as if old age had become a grateful retreat from unpleasant realities, a curtain one could drop at will to shut out the things one despised. In this curtained chamber of age one could stare at a son's wife and say, "I do not know you. You cannot touch me. I am old. No one exists in this rare air but Stephen and Lotta and Sophie. I have forgotten all unimportant things. You cannot deny me the joy of forgetting you."

"I'm not Hannah!" Cecily would exclaim. "Why does she always forget my name? She never forgets yours, Stephen."

"Stephen is my son," said Grandmother Truelove placidly.

Anna Stacey sat next to George with her shoulders crouched as if on an instant she would spring up and run. On the other side of the table Lynn and Sophie sat, and Anna could not eat for hating the carved perfection of Sophie's face, and the lazy adoration in Lynn's eyes. It was wicked for a woman to be so beautiful. It was wicked. It was unjust. Out of sheer perversity the blood would creep away from Anna's deathly lips and torment the end of her nose. When George tentatively sought her hand under the table, her nails dug into his palm until somewhat abashed he hurriedly withdrew his hand. ("I will shake her," he promised himself sullenly. "When we are married, I will be master.") Her thin shoulders tantalized his fingers and he set his lips grimly.

From Anna to Sophie there passed little threads of antagonism, and sometimes Sophie would lower her eyes at the sly knowledge in Anna's glance. Was a name written on her face, Sophie wondered, that Anna should make her voiceless inquisition? And then Stephen's hearty blustering voice would fling a tent of geniality over these feuds and discords, and Cecily, chirruping and clucking, decorated slumbering hates with trivialities. "More beef; George, you are pale today. Keep out in the sun more. . . . There, there, Custer, don't cry over spilled milk, for goodness' sake."

"Hannah, indeed! She does that on purpose to hurt me," Cecily was thinking, and then—"Now, Mother, do have a little more pudding. It won't do you a bit of harm."

Names, jests, were tossed about like gay serpentines to persuade a festival atmosphere, and these brilliant streamers were clung to with desperate joviality lest there be a gaunt silence and one's naked thought should stalk across the table.

"Jerome Gardiner will stay on the farm till Thanksgiving," said George, "We saw him in town yesterday at Clem's."

Sophie dared not look up.

"I don't see why you don't put alfalfa on that south thirty," said Stephen to Lynn, and Sophie was sick with disappointment that Jerome's name should have vanished. She looked desolately out the window. Would it be forever like this—that she must sit back, her passion folded demurely in her heart, waiting, continually waiting, for other hands to release it? She wanted to shout a name and hear it echoed a thousand times. She wanted to see him once more and burn from his touch. She closed her eyes and invoked the excitement of his presence. Her hands involuntarily gripped the table. When she opened her eyes she saw Anna Stacey smiling at her, a smile grooved on porcelain, hard, triumphant, knowing—a smile that had been born when Sophie Truelove went white at the mention of one man's name.

"Sophie, you must eat," scolded Cecily. "Just look at her, Lynn. She doesn't eat a thing."

"I'm not hungry," said Sophie, and looked away from Anna Stacey's eyes.

Early in November Stephen had to go to the city to buy a thresher, and Lynn went with him. Cecily wanted Sophie to stay at the Truelove farm over the one night, but Sophie wanted to be alone. What would it be to lie alone at night without Lynn's arms? Sophie saw herself torn with dim tenderness for her absent bridegroom. Alone she would be sure of one vivid need—

the need for Lynn. She remembered the nights after their first meeting when she had wished only for him—to see him again. Now to be alone in his house with his intimate things about her, her need for him would isolate itself from the chaos of her thoughts, would dominate her once again and give her peace.

He left at sunrise. As soon as the sound of the buggy wheels died Sophie sat weakly down on the porch steps, her eyes wide in disaster. If he should not come back—there might be an accident!—if she were to lose him forever! Her breath caught sharply, thinking of the misery of ever being without Lynn, of lonely nights puzzling over her desire.

It was strange, the sense of being alone in Lynn's house. Yet, after a while, she thought, how completely she filled it. It was her house, its walls were built for her, its roof to hold her gently prisoner until Lynn came back for her.

"I ought to feel that Lynn is here, though, even when he is away," thought Sophie.

His old hat and coat hanging on the kitchen rack, they should *be* Lynn to her. His boots leaning against the stove, his magazine spread out on the table—they should be Lynn, and should hold her as tightly as his own strong arms. It frightened her that she could not conjure him from his belongings, that they should be only an old hat, a coat, a pair of boots, a magazine. He was gone as completely as if he had never existed, as if she had always been alone. It was her house. Hers alone. A kitchen here where Sophie Truelove baked, a living room where Sophie Truelove embroidered her loneliness into monograms and scallops, a parlor with no funereal traditions but fresh with Sophie Truelove's ferns and geraniums. Upstairs rooms dark waiting for Sophie's imagination to give them significance. Rooms dark upstairs. Rooms dark upstairs with doors shut. In her mind Sophie turned their doorknobs fearfully. . . .

Lynn was gone and with him all security. Sophie got to her feet. . . . She must not, she would not open those dark rooms, she must not turn her head, she must not let that lustrous shadow come to life in her brain.

When night came she sat by the window, unable to work. Outside there was no moon or stars. A patter of drizzling rain beat monotonously on the roof, and the wind blew the tree branches about. The sad night wore on, and Sophie at the window, breathed more quickly. An impulse possessed her to feel that wet wind on her upturned face, to run away, to leave her walls and those dark rooms waiting upstairs for her.

"Lynn wouldn't want me to," she hesitated, her hand on a dark shawl. No, Lynn wouldn't want her to go out, to be alone with the night. The way Bert never wanted Mary Cecily to be alone with her music. The way Mother never wanted Father to stare into the fire, his pipe idle in his fingers. . . . There were things people could not understand about other people. It was no use. Things one must do. Things one couldn't explain. . . . Sophie jerked the shawl down and caught it over her shoulders. She ran out the door and into the welcoming blackness. The smell of wet chrysanthemums and rotting leaves embraced her.

Fear pounded ecstatically at her heart, beat inside her as she hurried along through the wet grass. She must not acknowledge to herself . . . she must never think . . . she must not say, "Why am I running toward that road, why am I straining my ears for horse's footfalls, why must I do this, and what is it that I must do?"

The wind was chilly and blew her black hair about her face. A dim moon emerged from a cloud and dangled among the pine-tops. Sophie heard a faint whinny and saw against the moonlight the outline of a horse. She was conscious of her feet hurrying on, of her cold hands being whipped by damp bushes, of someone catching her wrists, and then arms about her, and a dark face above her. She knew Jerome Gardiner would be there waiting for her . . . she had always known it. . . .

"You'd have to come sometime," his voice was softly exultant. "I was sure of that."

Sophie could not speak. It was folly to protest against his embrace since she knew now that it was for this she had come. It seemed to her that her body had become choked with tears, that this persistent dripping on the soggy earth was not rain but her own tears falling. His arms about her bore no comfort, only a sweet lacerating joy.

"I knew this would happen someday," she heard him say, "If I had to ride up to your door and take you. Sophie—Sophie, why have you been so long?"

"But I don't know why I came," she said forlornly. "I don't know why."

They walked along the road, his arm about her, Sophie's head turned so that it pressed back against his shoulder. Why, why was she here? There was no sound but the drip-drip of rain from the trees, the wet low branches beating against their faces, and the horse's feet sucking through the mud behind them. The moon had drawn a cloud again over her face, and they were in blackness, their feet hurrying along blindly. They passed the low rustic bridge, heard the lapping of water underneath, and felt wet slimy things underfoot. The wind hung about, chilly, macabre. Sophie turned once and saw a round drop of light through the trees. The light from her window, from the window of her lost white house.

Sophie shut her eyes. Jerome's arms tightened about her. She could hear him, under his breath, "God, how can people live wanting each other so much . . . belonging to each other. . . ." She was frightened of him, frightened of the agony his closeness brought to her. And he was afraid of her. They drew tighter to each other that the blackness should not come between them. She could feel his heart storming against hers. When the wind trailed haunting wet fingers against their faces, they both gasped. They were afraid. As if they two were alone on some desolate planet, frightened of each other, yet drawn together by their terror.

"We belong together, darling," Jerome breathed. "You knew it, too."

"I knew," Sophie's voice sounded far-off to her. Was this really she, after all, this wanton with her hair blowing wet against her face, running along midnight roads? Was not the real Sophie back there in that house in her husband's arms, beautifully cold and true?

They pushed against a gate into an enclosure. Behind them the horse stood still. Sophie stumbled and knew that it was a headstone her foot had tripped on. The graveyard . . . the darkness was spotted with nebulous gleaming shadows, monuments, tombstones. . . . And then Jerome's lips were upon hers. Her knees gave way before his strength. The cold marble beneath her was marvelously grateful to her burning flesh. Her fingers closed on cool myrtle leaves. The wind hung over them for a moment.

"Sophie . . . darling . . ."

Her body whirred. There was a singing in her veins. It was unendurable.

Lamps were still burning downstairs when Lynn came home soon after sunrise. He could see their gleam from the driveway, and frowning, tossed the reins over the teams' back and hurried into the house. The kitchen shades were drawn and the stove was cold. Sophie had not been down this morning. Lynn hesitated in the doorway to the sitting room, looking uneasily about him, one hand resting against the doorjamb. He walked over to the fat blue china lamp and turned down the wick. On the red fringed tablecloth Sophie's embroidery was a white crumpled heap.

Lynn squared his shoulders and strode over to the staircase, mounted the stairs. Odd Sophie wasn't downstairs to meet him, he thought. Over her doorknob his hand fumbled. She was his—his wife. It puzzled him that he should always hesitate before her door, as if she were only a guest in his house. Then he entered.

The early sun was trickling through the half-closed shutters into the room. It vibrated across the blue woven rug to the bed. In its path lay a dark shawl. Lynn picked it up. It was damp.

On the bed, face downward, and still as a corpse, Sophie lay fully dressed. Lynn touched her shoulder. In his inexplicable relief at finding her there he forgot his troubled misgivings.

"Sophie . . ."

Sophie turned her white face toward him. Inside her something seemed heavy and numb. All she could feel was the need for Lynn's arms. When he gently drew her into them she knew that never had her love for him burned with such a clear white radiance as now when she had put a world between them.

"What is it, dear? Were you afraid?"

"I was afraid," said Sophie in a tired monotone, "I sat up late and then. . . ."

"Poor little girl," Lynn patted her shoulder. "I must never leave you alone again."

"No, Lynn, you must never leave me again," whispered Sophie.

Lynn shook out the damp shawl he had hung over the chair. He wondered why Sophie had gone out in the rain.

It is a dreadful thing, Sophie thought, for a woman to live with two men, to lie in one man's arms and think of other arms, to smile into Lynn's clear eyes and see other eyes, dark and eager. Dreadful to feel that there is in the world something stronger than oneself, something that might leap out any minute and devour one's peace.

"This is not love," she insisted monotonously to herself. "There is only one love. There can only be one love, and I love Lynn."

She must not think of that night in the graveyard, of herself and Jerome at the gate long after midnight in each other's arms, half-sobbing because they must not meet again. "It would be destruction, dearest," she had whispered, frightened at the exultation in her body, an exultation to be reconstructed whenever their eyes met or their fingers touched. "This must be the end as well as the beginning," she said. Jerome had protested, implored, but she had shaken her head unhappily. "I am afraid . . . afraid. . . ." she had sighed. It could not be love, this thing that had made her forget her own soul. . . . He had stood at the gate long after she had fled up the pathway to her house.

Ah, no, there must be no remembering. She must control this shameful singing in her blood that should be remorse. She must wall this man's memory in a secret place where she would not dare to look. . . . Before Lynn she felt veiled and silent. It was agony to talk to him, because all words must pass that threshold sentence, the sentence that must never be said but would always stand there waiting between them. She knew Jerome had left for Washington again, and it might be months before he returned. They might never meet again. She must learn to be strong enough to wish that.

Then Mary Cecily and Robert came on the farm to wait till Bert's new home for them was ready, and Sophie was glad to find escape in the family living room from her own reproachful walls.

One day the three women were sitting by the fire, sewing, and talking of safe familiar things. Grandma Truelove sat in her chair in the corner, a little more shriveled, a little more removed from the world about her. ("How useless for women to talk," she was thinking, "How useless for women to sew! How useless for them to marry and bear children and talk and sew!")

Upstairs Robert was napping, but Lotta's children never napped. Now they sat at Cousin Tom's card table playing casino, and Lois scolded Custer for cheating, calling upon her elders for moral pressure, and Vera listened to what the women talked about and thought, "In a little while I will go upstairs. Everyone will think I've gone to take a nap. I can look in Mary Cecily's suitcase and in her dresser drawers."

"It will be nice to live in town, Mary Cecily," said old Cecily, her needle darting in and out of the guimpe she was embroidering for Lois's Sunday serge. "You will miss the cattle and the quiet but perhaps there will be other things for you in town. I've never cared for the city, myself."

The city. No, Cecily would never like cities. Cities or hotels or red, gilt rooms. A little shiver went through her. No, she would never like cities. . . .

"Lotta always liked cities," mused Grandma Truelove. "Lotta was made for cities. Perhaps I might have liked them, too. I never saw Washington."

Cecily bit off a thread.

"Doctor Gardiner has been to Washington every year," she said. "He says he wouldn't live there if you gave him the town."

Grandma smiled faintly, recognizing Cecily's gentle thrust at Lotta's judgment.

"Pooh, what does he know about it," she retorted. "I know those Gardiner men. The doctor and Ezra before him."

"Very brilliant men," said Cecily firmly.

"Weak," declared Grandma Truelove. "Weak with women. Every one of them."

"No," came faintly from Sophie's mouth. It must not be true that Jerome took other women as he had taken her. It should not be that her surrender was to him a casual thing. There must be no one for him but Sophie—never, never. She could not bear that any other woman should possess him. No, no, she kept repeating, confused, suffering.

"I'm sure the Gardiners are very clever men," said Cecily, taking Sophie's protests as purely amiable. "Mary Cecily went to school with Jerome before his father sent him away. A nice little fellow, wasn't he?"

"Yes," said Mary Cecily, leaning back in her chair, her eyes closed in the fatigue of conversation. She was thinking, "He says he will never buy me a piano, that it is bad for me. Tomorrow I will get out all the music and play and play until my wrists ache and the back of my head thrums and the end of my spine . . . Tomorrow and next day and the day after that."

Lois was sliding down from her chair. She came over to lean against her grandmother's lap.

"I will bring you a drink, Grandma," she said agreeably.

"Lois is a good child," said Cecily.

Lois tiptoed to the kitchen, flirting her skirts from side to side. She was a good child. She was getting grandmother a drink without even being asked. She was kind to old people. She would write a letter to Mother in Washington and tell her how Custer ate a worm and would die, and that Vera cut all the buttons off her new dress.

"Lynn is a good husband, isn't he," said Mary Cecily suddenly. "He said he would buy you a piano at Christmas time, when his uncle had sold some of the woodland. Just think, Sophie, you will have a piano."

"Lynn is a good husband," said Grandma Truelove. "They will have fine children."

"Yes, Lynn is kind," said Sophie in a low voice. She would not think of Jerome. She would not let him into her mind. She would never see him again. No matter how he pleaded, no matter how strong he was, she would never see him again. (But she *must* see him again!) She would not forget that Lynn was her true husband. (But she *would* forget Lynn!) She would never again yield herself to that black lust that made of wet sunken gravestones a warm and lovely couch. . . .

"I must go," said Sophie, springing to her feet. "I must see Lynn."

"But he said he would come by for you before supper," protested her mother. "Don't you feel well, Sophie? See, she has a fever."

"No, I'm all right," Sophie tried to laugh. It was not safe to be away from Lynn. Her heart was pounding—if she should see him again . . . if she should see *him*. . . .

"John has just gotten back from town. He can drive you back before he unhitches," said Cecily. "You're quite sure you feel well, Sophie?"

She wondered if Sophie were going to have a child. She acted queerly. You had to humor young wives.

"She will own a piano," thought Mary Cecily, looking after her. "Her husband is not afraid of her."

Vera slid back into her chair at the card table. No one noticed her absence. Her sister, busy in helping Custer build a card house, looked at her sternly.

"Someone has been eating wintergreen," she announced in a clear voice.

"There is some in my telescope," said Mary Cecily. "I brought it for Grandmother. It's in a paper bag right on top. Run and get it, Vera."

"I'm afraid of waking Bobby," said Vera regretfully. She hadn't meant to eat it all. Just one or two pieces.

"You're a thoughtful little girl," said Mary Cecily. "When Bobby wakes up, then, you may have one of the wintergreen candies."

Vera coughed and would not meet her sister's malicious glance.

Bert was a thick, square, silent man. He was like his father, who had owned a factory in Defiance. When his father died, people thought, "Die? How could he die when he was made of steel and granite?" Bert was like that. He had won Mary Cecily by planting his granite body in her path, his feet propped apart, and when she would have fluttered past him, his steel arms closed around her. He took her away and put her in a house with white blowing curtains and bowls of yellow lilies in the windows.

Mary Cecily was happy with him, for she belonged nowhere and to no one but bore her own happiness about with her, complete in itself. Bert was to her a formless gray reassuring rock on which one stood. He was Husband. Mary Cecily had not the faintest curiosity about him except when her baby was born and he sat beside her white still bed with his granite shoulders shaking. Then a vague wonder stirred her, and she put her hand out curiously to touch him, as if perhaps there might be some reality in him after all.

He did not exist in her world, and sometimes she was aware of his misery in being left out. Then she was sorry and grave and said to herself, "I must tell him things. I must tell him that today I am going to walk far out the east road and find a beechwoods. But what shall I say when he asks me why?" So she said nothing, but smiled and was sorry she could not open her doors to him.

Sometimes Bert could not bear her beautiful remoteness. When she played the piano at her father's house and never heard him or saw him there beside her, smiling with wide glittering eyes right through him. . . . Then he would take her two hands and pull her away from the piano back to him.

When the new house—it was to be in town—was finished he came up to the Truelove farm to take Mary Cecily and the boy home. As he walked up to the house, carpetbag in hand—John and George unhitching out by the stable door—Robert ran screaming out to meet him and Mrs. Truelove took off her apron and came to the door to welcome him. But Mary Cecily did not come out. Bert could hear the tinkle of the piano from the parlor window, and coldness settled on his face. He kissed Mrs. Truelove, and his son perched jubilantly on his shoulders, strode toward the parlor. He stopped in the doorway but Mary Cecily did not look up. Her hands fondled the keys and her blonde head was bent low over them, as if listening to notes between notes, melodies hidden under other melodies.

"Bert's here," called Cecily.

"She doesn't care," Bert said in a husky monotone. "She's crazy about that music. It's bad for her, I tell you, Mother. When a woman gets so excited over a piano that she can't see her own husband . . . I tell you I won't have it. I tell you, it's making her queer."

Mary Cecily went on playing, breathless, flushed, immersed. Her mother's thin face became white with an unacknowledged terror, and then relentlessly she drew the curtains of her thought. Mary Cecily was a Mills and the Mills were quiet, safe, people.

"She's always loved music," she said in a commonplace voice.

Mary Cecily looked up suddenly.

"Why, Bert!" she said.

He put down Robert and came over to her. He pulled her up from the piano stool, and dropped the lid over the keys. Silently he locked it, Mary Cecily looking at him, sorry for him, sorry because he couldn't understand, sorry because he was so far, far away.

"I don't want you to play anymore," he said. "Ever."

"I won't," said Mary Cecily, still sorry for him.

But she went around the house with a restless unhappiness for the next few days. She must not touch the piano, because music flung a towering wall between herself and her husband. Her fingers burned for the cool keys. She ached with the desire to pluck lovely sounds from the air with her two hands. . . . Bert watched her sullenly, wretchedly. She was very kind to him, because she was sorry for him, more than ever now that he was making her suffer. There was a bright glaze over her blue eyes, and an air of secret contentment hung about her as if the piano after all meant nothing to her, as if Bert need not reproach himself for denying her music, because see how happy she was without it. See how she could smile, see how tender she could be, see how completely she had forgotten his cruelty!

For days the piano remained locked. Bert became jovial, even jaunty. He tossed Robert—ecstatic—into the air, carried Custer and Vera (she was a yellow-haired lady in a spangled dress on a marching white horse) on his shoulders. But Mary Cecily wandered desolately about the house, her fingers locked together, but smiling steadily.

One morning before even Bessie was up Mary Cecily arose and waked little Robert to go with her for a walk in the dew.

"But I'm hungry, Mother," drowsily confessed Robert, extending thin little arms to be poked into sleeves. "Shan't we eat breakfast first?"

Mary Cecily laughed at him in a hushed excited way and carried him in her arms tiptoe out of the house. The sky was ashes and a gray mist veiled the trees and stables. The tail of a night wind scuttled through the tall orchard grass. The cattle made no sound in the barn nor were the roosters aware that dawn was smoldering behind the horizon blotted with pine trees. Robert, a little sleepy, a little excited, ran along beside his mother, his hand tight in her thin fingers. Mary Cecily was very happy. She moved swiftly through the meadow, her full skirts swishing against the weeds, stiff with cold dew, and she sang in a breathless low voice.

"That's Grandmother's song," rebuked Robert. He had seen a small gray bird asleep on a branch. Birds did sleep.

Mary Cecily laughed and squeezed his hand. They passed John's still hut and followed the bushy path by the creek. The water splashed over miniature falls and stepping-stones in low purling octaves and arpeggios.

"It sings," said Robert.

"Of course it does," Mary Cecily cried delightedly. Now it was all Robert's short legs could do, skipping and running, to keep up with his mother's swift stride. The creek grew wider and wider. There were no more stones in it and it had the tranquillity of depth. Its purl had become a low deep hum, and Mary Cecily, bending over it a moment, laughed aloud.

"Do you hear it?" she demanded.

Robert nodded, quite out of breath from his scurrying. He could hear it. Like the sounds the organ made before the notes separated. Muffled light broke through the gray of the sky, but there was no sun. Beyond the hill, a cock pompously cleared his throat. Mary Cecily began to run along the path, Robert scrambling after her.

"I can hear it, too, can't I?" he panted anxiously.

"Wait till we get to the dam," said his mother, and squeezed his fingers tightly.

On they hurried until there could be heard the roar of water hurtling down over rocks and foam went spinning out in whirling wheels. Above the dam the water was still and deep with no ripple on its silken surface.

Mary Cecily stood still and Robert's yellow head drooped against her skirts.

"The music's gone, hasn't it, mother?" he inquired disappointedly.

"No," breathed Mary Cecily. "It's underneath. Listen."

But Robert could not hear. He sat down on the edge of the bank and watched his mother patiently. Mary Cecily stood at the edge of the water, bending a little forward, straining her ears. There was music underneath, sometimes the melody glanced her ear—almost—almost she could hear it. She *must* hear it. Her fingers spread apart as though for waiting octaves. The sun struggling through the gray sky, flung a quivering golden staircase down into the river—to its very bottom. Mary Cecily took a step. Radiantly she walked into the water, following the elusive stairs. The riverbed dropped abruptly a few feet from the edge. Mary Cecily found the bottom of the stairs. . . . In a moment great chords were bursting about her head. Church organs pealed and angels on stained glass windows sang ravishing hymns.

The sun emerged triumphant and commanded color. The sky became marvelously blue and shadows in fields became rust-color or antique green. Robert sat on the bank by the dam for a long time but his mother did not come back. After a while he was hungry and trudged back home across the fields.

Windows in the Truelove house stared bleakly at the harvest. A curtain blew out here and was a shroud. Desolate eyes peered from the darkened rooms at November dawns and dusks. Women in black scurried in from the well and hid from daylight; there was no laughter. They spoke of other things but death peered through the lattice of their conversation. Mary Cecily was dead and Bert had run from the house, his son on his shoulders, and they would never see little Robert again.

There had been that morning after the suicide when Bert had locked himself in the parlor and with his own hands torn to shreds every sheet of music. There had been that afternoon when

Stephen had found Cecily down by the creek, her apron over her head, convulsed with sorrow. "My people aren't like that," she had wept, "Mary Cecily was mine, not yours or your mother's." There had been Bessie wailing at her work and Sophie, dry-eyed, whispering, "I wish I could do that. I wish it had been I!" And in the granary Lotta's three children sat in an empty bin and bitterly envied the vanished Robert his distinction.

"We must shut the door," Stephen said one day. "People cannot grieve forever. We must not think of her."

It occurred to him then that a new daughter in the house might give Cecily something new upon which to fasten her mind. He urged George to marry immediately and bring Anna Stacey to the house. So, soon after Thanksgiving, George and Anna were quietly married in the Anderson parlor with only Stephen and the two old maids as witnesses. No one guessed that Anna Stacey's triumph galled her more than it did even the Anderson girls.

Sophie's own room was given to the bride and groom, and the maple branches that had heard Sophie Truelove's mute prayers now heard a man's conquering lovemaking, with a woman's whispered interpolation—"I hate you, I hate you—I hate you!" Sometimes in the darkness George got up and lit a candle to study curiously the marks of teeth on his arm, or to bandage a bruised wrist. In the candlelight Anna sat up in bed, her thin arms hugging her knees, her mouth twisted in triumph. Not until she was finally asleep did George dare to lie down beside her, and then he touched her slight shadowy figure apprehensively, and fell asleep with amazement etched on his face.

In the daytime Anna followed Cecily about the house with murmured offers of help in this or that domestic chore. Cecily did not want to be unkind, but she hated assigning the little duties that had been Sophie's to this odd creature George had married. Grandmother Truelove withdrew into a pleasant twilight that obscured sorrow and the unpleasant details of life such as Cecily, George's bride, and John's dogs. Anna Stacey knew the old woman watched her reflecting, "What is this strange woman doing in my house? What right has she under the Truelove roof?"

Anna was nervous and unhappy, but before Dora Hamilton and the Anderson girls she allowed herself certain arrogant gestures. Marriage was nothing, she assured them. Absolutely nothing. If it hadn't been for George's importunings she would have preferred—really Lucy, honestly Sara!—to go on teaching in the Ridge school. A man was a nuisance, you know. . . . She wrote home to Steubenville that she had finally made a choice among her suitors, and henceforth please address all mail to Mrs. George Truelove, Ashton County. She hoped Clara was having fun with her telegraph operators and dispatch clerks. Personally she never had any use for railroad men.

There was really nothing to do since Cecily Truelove refused her help, but to make over old dresses, embroider towels, and to engage in vicious silent combats with her new husband. Finally Cecily, on a suggestion from Grandmother Truelove, permitted her to go through certain old trunks, retrieving pieces of lace and bolts of cloth that might be of use. Anna sat in the storeroom shaking out old garments and trying on the lesser-worn ones. It was ridiculous, she thought, being Mrs. Truelove and having no more clothes than she had owned as Anna Stacey. She wanted rose-colored satins with trains and silver buttons and black velvet gowns with passementerie and gold lace.

Cecily said, "I am sending to the Columbus store for samples of dress goods. I think a brown broadcloth would be nice for you and a good quality poplin for dress. Plum-color, say."

"Yes," said Anna, twisting her hands.

She wanted pink and baby blue in ruffles and lace with fancy braid, so she would look soft and smoothly feminine like Sophie

Truelove. Then resentful tears came to her eyes, remembering that she had always wanted fluffy things and when she wore them people always laughed at her.

"Not your style, Anna," Dora Hamilton used to chuckle. "You look just like a picked chicken."

There were things in the trunks, however, that Anna eagerly appropriated. Stiff yellowed taffeta petticoats with a hundred ruffles. Brocaded velvets that Grandmother Truelove had worn. Anna would sit on the little low chair that had been Sophie's with a heap of salvaged costumes on her lap and rip and snip absorbedly. (How chagrined Hart Purvis would be when he saw how pretty she was in crimson velvet! How Lynn would stare when he saw her at Sunday dinner in this gorgeous satin! "What? Is this the woman I turned from to speak to Sophie Truelove one day?" How alluring she would be!) Tom and Stephen sat at the table playing patience while George looked on. (Would she ever look up at him? He didn't dare look at her again because Grandma's eyes were upon him with shrewd understanding. Besides she never would look up at him. Unless he struck her. Unless he hit her with the back of his hand across her cruel tight little mouth.)

Cecily fluttered in and out from the kitchen. She was setting bread. She would not think of Mary Cecily. She would not think of her. Now she had a new daughter. A nice quiet little woman. A good wife for George. She must learn to like her. She must stop and say kind things to her from time to time. ("How do you plan to fix this, Anna? Drawn up on the side that way? Very pretty. You must ask Bessie to help you when you come to the stitching.") She must not let Grandmother Truelove see her brush away a tear. Grandmother Truelove would say, "The Mills women have no backbone. Never had. We Trueloves—(Why did she always call herself a Truelove, as if she had been born one?)—are used to bearing our griefs like gentlewomen. When

Nathan died I didn't allow myself to shed one tear. Nathan always admired my character."

Stephen, too, thought of the new daughter in the house and occasionally turned to her with some grave inquiry. She would look up at him with half-defiant, half-scared eyes, and make guarded answers. A queer mousy little creature with sharp little teeth like a fox. He wondered why George had selected her when there were pretty buxom black-eyed girls all over the county waiting for husbands. The Cole girls, for example. . . . When Tom got up once to stretch his legs Stephen came over to Anna's side. She was tearing a seam in a dress with her scissors. At Stephen's approach she held up a yellow envelope with a sly smile.

"This was in the petticoat pocket," she informed him. "It must be pretty old, too. Almost falling apart."

"What is it, Anna?" asked Cecily, coming in from the kitchen. Stephen was holding up the envelope and Cecily's heart turned. Stephen looked at the envelope a long time and studied the torn scraps of paper inside it.

"Do you know what this is?" he slowly asked his wife.

Cecily looked at him piteously, one hand clutching her withered old throat.

"I—you see—I didn't want you to have it, Stephen," she gasped all in a breath. To her surprise Stephen was not angry. He tapped the letter gently with his forefinger. (Kate had written. Lotta had said so, too. She had cared.)

"Not that it matters now," he said, "Not in the least my dear. Not in the very least."

He walked back to the card table. Cecily found herself looking into her daughter-in-law's mocking inscrutable face. Anna knew. Anna knew now what the Anderson girls had always known. She had come—was there no mercy?—to bring more misery into an old woman's life. Cecily's lips trembled.

She took off her glasses and wiped them carefully on her apron. Anna went on snipping with deliberate absorption, but Cecily understood her. She must face that veiled contempt, that mocking sympathy, day in and day out for weeks, months, years. She hated her son's wife. Oh, how wretched the years would be! Three people now under one roof knowing a certain thing, thinking of one dead woman—no better than a courtesan, she was!—Cecily shut her eyes tightly at this dreadful glimpse of the future.

"I must go and tell Bessie to remember my biscuits in the morning," she murmured, and walked slowly out into the hall, one hand groping for the wall, like a blind person.

How much better to be dead, Sophie thought, than to be afraid of oneself! What had Mary Cecily to die for, she wondered? What had she, Sophie, to live for except eternal suffering? To belong to two men and therefore to no one, not even to herself . . . she could not leave Lynn because she loved him. Yet the instant Jerome should beckon her—Would he, she asked herself?—No, no! She must struggle to command her emotions. She must learn to dominate her own heart.

Nights that Lynn went to town meetings Sophie would walk endlessly across the black frost-flecked meadows hunting peace. Sometimes tears would blur her eyes and she told herself she was grieving for Mary Cecily. But she knew it was not for her dead sister, but for herself she grieved, that she envied Mary Cecily her final safety.

Hurrying across the frosted stubble, her shawl wrapped about her, her hair blown back from her forehead, she could see the darkness pierced by lights on far hills. She knew that each light meant a fireside, a dozing husband, a tranquil wife knitting beside him, children asleep upstairs under sloping eaves. She pitied and envied those women their serenity. She envied, too, whatever young girl leaned out the dormer window upstairs, and made a wish on a falling star. She would wish—how well Sophie knew!—that the blue-eyed stranger she saw today on the post office steps would ask someone her name, would seek her out and carry her away to a white cottage. A white cottage with green shutters. Each night she would make her wish on a shooting star, on a four-leaf clover, a snow-white horse, on the petals of a flower, until one day he would come for her—these things did happen! He would carry her away, and they would be happy, they would be a light flickering across dark frosted fields, they would be a light symbolizing peace and tranquil love.

For her, for that young girl, there would be no unwanted ghosts to tap upon her bedroom window, there would be—for that tranquil bride, no tom-tom of unfulfillment beating in her heart, no crazy shadows to drag her across dark graves at night. She would sit beside her dozing husband and be happy. Sophie Truelove alone, in all this world, must find no peace, must be blown by chilly night winds across bleak fields and frozen ditches, needing this love and craving that.

Twice in her wanderings Sophie came to the graveyard, and once to the edge of her own father's farm, a ghost visiting the scene of its past life. It seemed to her that her feet were digging into the soil to assure their footing, that if she did not hold to this fence rail the wind would waft her lightly into air again. Once a team and wagon passed her and then she was conscious of her reality, that she was a woman alone on the road at night. She crouched behind a tree until the farmer had passed.

She would not say this to herself but some night she would, she knew, meet Jerome. He had gone to Washington again but during his father's sickness he might come back. Senator Anderson's wife lived in Washington. Would he see her? Would there be other women in Washington, women he would crush in his arms and consume? "The Gardiner men are weak with women," Grandmother Truelove had said. She could not endure that there should be anyone else. Even sleeping in Lynn's arms, she could not bear to think of Jerome possessing any other woman. Yet, she thought, he could never be anything to her. She had Lynn, and in a little while she would forget Jerome. She would learn to hear his name and be unmoved, to see his face, his dark eyes, and to be casual, to—yes, to touch his hand and remain smiling and serene. She would be as sure of herself as she was of Lynn, for how could one be happy knowing that any breeze might uproot one? As for Jerome—perhaps he did not care. Their night, perhaps, meant nothing, else how could he have stayed away so long—no matter how she had begged him to, he would have ignored her fears and come to her somehow. He was weak with women. She had been only another for him. Very well, when he returned to Ashton she would bow to him as if nothing had happened. She would even invite him to call and be politely composed. She would indeed. He could have written to her—yet how could he have written? He might have come back another day and said—what could he have said? . . . . No, it was as she had said it must be, the end as well as the beginning. Two strangers they were and must remain, two strangers caught in a curious passion that must die since it could not be denied. . . . She would never go to him again. She would even visit the graveyard and smile aloofly at her own folly. . . .

Lynn went to a town meeting and Sophie, a little later, was walking swiftly across the meadows until she recognized the mulberry tree at the foot of her father's fields. The moon was a wisp above the bare trees and sent a trickle of pale light over the earth. The women were at the farmhouse—Sophie could see their lamp-lit windows—but John and the men had gone to the meeting. She dared not think of what she would have to say if someone should meet her now, if Bessie should chance to run down to John's hut for a farm journal, if Anna or her mother should have some errand at the spring house. On the eastern hill she caught sight of a figure silhouetted against the moon. Someone was coming toward her. Sophie stopped short, but in another moment she knew that it was Jerome and that he had seen her. It was her opportunity to turn and flee, to purge herself by denial. He was coming toward her swiftly. She must turn back now. Quick, she must turn and run. She must not meet him, must not hear his voice, must not touch him. . . .

They met at the foot of the hill.

In the hut a single candle glowed and sputtered. It flared against the windowpanes and rafters but left the corners in a hush of darkness.

She was quiet in his arms. He stroked her hair and kissed her wet eyelids. He was tormented with desire for her, desire that the surrender of her body did not appease. Here, limp in his arms, with this aching tenderness between them, she was as remote as the lady in the moon, her white passion left him savagely frustrated.

"It isn't love," she whispered. "I know it isn't love."

"Sophie, darling, do we know what it is?" Jerome asked sadly. "Are you so sure? We know—well, what?—that we can't bear to leave each other."

"I don't know what it is," murmured Sophie. "I'm afraid."

"Foolish . . ." his lips brushed hers.

Her head drooped against his shoulder. How little they had to say to each other, and yet this was exquisite understanding. There were things that should be said—that they must never meet again, and that they could bring no happiness to each other. . . . She saw her thoughts in his restless eyes. If he would tell her that this was the end of wonder, if he would say there could be no one else, if he would say that this was love. . . . But . . .

"How soft your hair is, darling," was all that he said.

$\mathcal{T}$HE REVEREND JEPSON—even in his blue night-shirt with his beard untrimmed he was still the minister—looked out of his bedroom window, saw that there had been no more snow and said to Elizabeth, his wife, "The roads will be splendid today, my dear. The church will be full. All of the farmers will come. We ought to collect enough for the Sunday school carpet." He hurriedly dressed and went downstairs, ate six griddlecakes and two eggs—"No coffee on the Sabbath, Elizabeth."

Walking across the slippery sidewalk to the churchyard, Bible in hand, he saw that already one horse and carriage stood by the hitching rail. He recognized the horse and wished—this was really not Christian, he reminded himself, really not decent—that more people would arrive quickly. Awful—not Christian to think this, at all, you know—to be forced to carry on a conversation indefinitely with those two old maids. They were good women and God had not seen fit to provide them with husbands. He should be kind and helpful to them in their lonely old age. They were good churchgoers. No matter how cold, nor how bad the roads they always came to church. He wondered sometimes if this were really wise. Suppose they contracted pneumonia sitting in his cold church, could he ever forgive himself?

The church at first glimpse seemed empty. After all it was quite early. Silence poured in the stained glass window and filled the aisles. In the eighth right-hand pew two green feathered discs vibrated, slowly lifted, and became eager pointed faces against green pancake hats.

"Good morning, Miss Lucy. Good morning, Miss Sara. Splendid Sabbath, today, is it not?"

(They clung to his hand so! They would ask him to tea again, and what could he say? Such horrid tea! Such soggy pancakes! But fine women, both of them. God's noblewomen. Why didn't someone come? Miss Purvis, now, the soloist. And why was Elizabeth so late? Surely it needn't take her all day to dress. She was putting on the roast, of course. . . .)

"You haven't been to see us for two week," coquetted Lucy. "Is that fair, Doctor Jepson?"

"We expected you for two Wednesdays," rebuked Sara, still clinging to his unhappy hand. "You must make up for it."

He laughed—did it sound weak and apologetic? He meant it to be healthy good nature.

"He must come for tea *and* dinner next Wednesday," said Lucy.

"Well, now, really Miss Lucy, that's being too good . . ." He prayed for a miracle.

There was Miss Purvis suddenly in her seat by the organ in gray with an ecstatic blue hat and long kid gloves, sufficient equipment for a soprano soloist.

"Oh, Miss Purvis, I must see you . . ."

He had never been so glad to see Miss Purvis before. He took both of her hands and shook them interminably. She lowered her eyes and thought, "He's only human, after all." And then more carriages and sleighs arrived and people poured in with deep

Sunday voices and solemn coughs. There would surely be enough in the collection plate, surely enough for the Sunday school carpet! The Coles, the Thompsons, the Mills, the Greers, the Trueloves, and finally Elizabeth hurrying in to the organ, her bonnet askew on untidy gray-streaked hair, and—merciful heavens!—her forgotten kitchen apron showing beneath her coat!

"We will sing Hymn Number 349," said the minister. To Sophie, he was only a little potbellied man in a big collar. An enormous collar. "Hymn Number 349. Come Thou Almighty King."

Sophie absently leafed the pages of the hymnbook. There were two pews for Trueloves but they were seldom filled. Today there were Stephen, George, John, Lynn and the two women, Sophie and Anna. Anna had developed a new arrogance from her new brown broadcloth with the red velvet hat and new city shoes. She was confident of her appearance until Sophie came, and then people had stopped, not to say, "How handsome you look, Anna! How stylish!" but to say, Anna's new beauty all unobserved, "How pale you are, Sophie! Are you ill?"

"Your hat looks mighty pretty," George whispered to his wife.

"Shut up!" she snapped. As if his praise meant anything to her.

"Come Thou Almighty King.

Help us thy name to sing. . . ." said the minister, one eye on Elizabeth. She was furiously thumbing the hymnbook, but there was no page 369—or what was it James had said?—She couldn't remember. 369—359—He would be annoyed. But everything in the world had slipped her mind as soon as she saw that greasy apron peeping up at her from under her coat. Page—page—

"Help us to praise. . . ."

Sophie looked out the stained glass window and thought of Jerome. In church! She hastily turned back to the page. Anna Stacey had slid behind George to her side to share the book. Sophie was absently conscious of a whisper in her ear but she forgot to answer. Anna had said—what was it? . . .

"Come Thou Almighty King, Hymn Number 349, Hymn Number 349."

The organ began. Miss Purvis opened her mouth and the blue roses on her blue velvet hat shook with expectant tremors. Elizabeth pumped stoutly on the organ and her plump fingers boldly essayed improbable octaves. (Had she put enough wood on the stove, she wondered? Had she put salt on the potatoes?)

Sophie thought, what had Anna Stacey said to her? It was unimportant but she should not have brushed her aside. What was it she had said? Their two thumbs holding the hymnbook almost touched.

"I saw you go into the hut that night," Anna whispered. "I was coming through the orchard. I saw you go in there with him."

"Come, Thou Almighty King,
Help us they na-a-ame to sing,
Help us to praise. . . ."

. . . voices began on a hundred different notes and merged into the one suggested by the organ. Sophie's lips moved but no sound came. She could not stand, no she could not, yet she dared not be weak. Someone—Anna Stacey—had seen her that night. . . . Sophie shivered.

"Slut!" said Anna Stacey in a breath and went on singing.

The Reverend Jepson looked over his flock and thought that never had he heard such glorious singing. Today one shrill joyous soprano voice dominated the whole congregation, even drowned out Gladys Purvis's invincible coloratura. It came from this side, he thought, yes from this side. He must find out who it was and compliment her on it afterwards, whoever she might be.

The fat blue china lamp sent important light over a wide-open, blue-lined ledger, and persuaded golden bubbles in the ink pot. Sophie kept one finger on the line that in her own careful handwriting said,

"Eggs at 82¢ a basket . . ."

and pondered stupidly over four times eighty-two. Four times two . . . She wondered if she were going to have a child. It was too soon to be certain. Eight. Four times eight . . . There it was. Three sixty eight. If she should have a child . . . if she should have a child . . .

"On the nineteenth only two baskets of eggs. Two times. . ."

"Saw your dad in town today," said Lynn—he was polishing his guns out by the kitchen stove. "He wanted to know why you hadn't been over lately. Your mother's sort of worried."

The pen stabbed at a golden bubble.

"The roads have been bad," said Sophie. "The snow and slush . . ."

She would have to go over to the farm. She could not keep away from Anna Stacey forever. But what should she say to her—how could she speak to her without fear trembling in her voice, fear at the dreadful thing Anna knew?

"George's wife isn't very good company, I guess," said Lynn.

"I suppose not," said Sophie. "Have you . . ." she dared not ask if Anna had hinted things to him. But how else was she to know whether he guessed. . . .

"I don't like the woman," said Lynn, preoccupied with his gun. "She has a sharp tongue, you know."

What had she said? What had she told? Sophie saw a small blot settling on her white, blue-lined page.

"Two times eighty-two . . ."

Lynn glanced up from his polishing now and then to smile at his wife bending absorbed over her bookkeeping. He wished that she would turn around so that he might see the puzzled, adorable line between her eyes. She would sit—he knew—with pen motionless for a long time, her head bending lower over her books, until presently he would tiptoe in, glance over her shoulder, and laughingly solve the problem that was taxing her. . . . How different she was from all other women! Yet after all, like his mother, he thought. . . . A mysterious person his mother had been, a woman with sleek yellow hair and a gentle tired smile. He could remember long ago sitting with his mother by the little brook past the clump of hickory trees. He was very small. . . . There had been a blue pebble near an ant hill and the ants running, running—lost then among enormous waving blades of grass.

"Look," said his mother, and he squatted by the stream and looked in it. Little tiny fish—"Minnows," said his mother—squirming through the water, and a thing at the very bottom—"A crawfish," she said—that waved its arms and legs a little and still could not swim.

"Nice, isn't it, Lynnie?" said his mother.

It had been a Sunday afternoon, now he remembered.

"Yes," he said, but he couldn't look up because suddenly there was a lady smiling up at him from the water. He put his hand in the water to touch the water-lady—"You can't catch the fish that way, Lynnie,"—and she went away. Then the ripples stopped and she was there again, beautifully smiling.

"What do you see, son?" asked his mother, and then he saw the water-lady's lips move and knew that it was his own mother. This lovely thing was his very own, he thought. His. No one could take her away. Not the fish nor the thing at the bottom, ("A crawfish," she had said). His . . .

"Come," she had said. "We must go back."

But he hung back a little because he did want to watch the fish, he said. . . . The next month his mother died. "It isn't fair," he told his aunt, bewilderedly. She had been his, you see, *his,* and people couldn't take away the things that were his.

Now he watched Sophie in the other room, her head bent over budget problems. She was his, he thought, his. . . . This exquisite dream could not vanish for he had held it in his arms. This perfection, this loveliness belonged to him, was tangible, was bound to him. His!

She was figuring raptly. "A mistake," he thought, and adored her stupidity. He would tiptoe behind her, find that she had added six and eight to make fifteen, and when he would quietly point to it she would laugh, lean her head against him, and the little lines between her eyes would vanish.

"I do make such silly mistakes, don't I, dear?" she would say.

He tiptoed through the door. Sophie, intent, did not hear him, and the pen scratched on slowly. Lynn stopped behind her chair and leaned over.

"Two baskets at 82¢ . . ." he read, and then—the pen went right on scratching dreamily—"Jerome Gardiner Jerome Gardiner Jerome Gardiner Jerome Gardiner . . ."

Lynn watched her writing the name again.

He tiptoed back to the chair by the kitchen stove, his brows drawn together.

Sophie sat on the footstool of her grandmother's chair, her soft blue wool gown spreading into the blue of the woven rug, into the staid folds of the old woman's black poplin skirt. They two were alone in the dusk as they had often been before, silent, close, with the fire licking the darkness of the chimney and sending reflections experimenting on polished chair backs.

She was a stranger here now, Sophie thought somberly, a stranger in an enemy's house. As long as Anna Stacey dwelt here she, Sophie, would be an alien. Anna was calling on the Purvis' today—Sophie had made sure of that before she came—and there was only her workbasket on the table to warn Sophie of the dangerous knowledge its owner cherished.

"Does she really know," Sophie's thoughts circled monotonously, "or has she guessed? Does anyone else know? Will she tell Lynn? What shall I say to her if she should accuse me again?"

She looked curiously at the bland serenity of her grandmother's face. There, surely, was one who had never known confusion. No doubts had ever perturbed her, no man, no woman's eyes. . . .

Cecily came in from the kitchen, nervously wiping her hands on a checked percale apron.

"Isn't she back yet?" she whispered.

Sophie shook her head, and her mother dropped into a chair, relief on her thin worn face.

"I don't like her, Sophie," she murmured with a cautious look over her shoulder. "I don't like her a bit, but of course I daren't let her see. George, either."

Sophie put her hand impulsively toward her mother.

"I don't like her, either," she breathed, and then looked back into the fire. "I—I don't know why."

Grandmother Truelove lifted her eyebrows, first at Sophie, then at Cecily. George's wife. That was the one they were talking of. The little tight thin creature with the scissors and pins in her mouth.

"She's nothing," she scoffed. Women not liking other women, she thought. Silly. Women were nothing. Hates were nothing.

"I don't know why," repeated Sophie.

"I can't sit here when she's home," Cecily said almost in a whimper. "It's just as if it were her house. I tell you I don't like her. I wish George would take her away."

"He never will," said Grandmother Truelove. "She'll be here until you die, Cecily Mills. When Stephen goes, she will have your room and you will have the little end room where I am. She will be the one to dry the corn and put up the cherries, and you will knit boots for her babies. I know."

She drew her shawl closer about her neck and smiled enigmatically at Sophie. Cecily's fingers clenched the arm of her chair but she did not answer. Stephen's mother was an old, old woman about to die. One must not answer her challenges.

"I don't like her," she said, "and I don't see what George finds in her."

"When you're as old as I am, Cecily Mills, you will see how silly you are," said Grandmother Truelove, "letting strangers bother you. Sitting here fretting about your son's wife. As if she were anything! You have a lot to learn, Cecily Mills, and it's time you were learning it."

She closed her eyes and retreated into the vague half-world that was her refuge.

Cecily went back to the kitchen. The old woman would die someday and she, Cecily, would be glad she had never said the things she felt. She would be proud that no taunt had ever left her lips. She would dress her painstakingly in black bombazine for a shroud, and no one would reproach her for shedding no tears. No one could hear the singing in her heart.

"Poor Mother," said Sophie.

"She's nothing," drowsed Grandmother Truelove. She was light as air now (with her eyes shut) only for the locket on her neck, the locket with Lotta's baby picture in it. That pricked her skin so that she blinked and saw the leaping fire and Sophie at her feet.

"Someday you will have a baby," she said to Sophie.

Sophie did not look up.

"Perhaps," she said in a low voice.

"A girl," said Grandmother Truelove contentedly. She fingered the locket at her throat. Lotta at eighteen months. Her baby. She could not die until she had seen Lotta again.

"Lotta is a pretty name for a little girl," she said.

"I will call her Lotta," promised Sophie.

"But if it's a boy?" anxiously asked her grandmother.

Sophie's head bent lower.

"I don't know," she murmured. "I don't know what name to give if it's a boy."

When she had said it she looked quickly around as if Anna Stacey's smile might mock her from the window or a doorway, but there was absolute peace in the room. She sighed. Grandmother Truelove's eyes stared at Sophie through the dusk. A smile slit her withered face and did not change. She knew that Sophie—or was it Lotta? or was it herself young?—sat at her feet with firelight flushing her skin, but she herself was retreating into a forest of shadows, and this person—was it Lotta? was it Sophie?—was nothing, the room was nothing, her hands on the arms of her chair felt no contact, a draft from a window blew a lock of hair against her neck but was neither cold nor warm, it was nothing. Trees, houses, snows were nothing, for she was a woman in a tomb with earth radiating from her fingers and a marble stone above her—heavy, heavy! .... The wind running through the grass tickled her but was not cold or warm for it was nothing. She was in a tomb, locked in the earth like a treasure, a gold locket with a baby's picture corroding her neck. It weighed on her—that gold locket—more than any tombstone, more than this mountain on her forehead, more than this ship-clogged ocean that throbbed against her feet. It dug through webs of clothing, through tucks of dried flesh, through bone, a cruel gold locket with a baby's picture inside. It drew her through rosewood, and earth and marble into space. She was a cloud. Tombstone weighing on an empty coffin now. She was a cloud spread far up against blue color with high sweet sounds pushing against her. Now she was blown against a hill—the cloud blurred into sky—melting shadowless to moss. Cool smooth tired moss—a gold locket lacerating her—. She was wind in a maple tree—lonely tomb and shrunken coffin!—she was breath on a windowpane, she was a sigh.

Firelight tantalized her shut eyes. Her fingers closed over the locket and it was cold. The draft from the doorway was cold. The hand on the wicker armchair was cold, even with miniature flames flickering in the old wedding ring. . . .

Petulantly she motioned Sophie to adjust her shawl.

Anna was in the doorway, drawing off her gloves, her nose triumphantly rosy under her red hat.

"Well, Sophie!" she said.

Sophie got up.

"Good-afternoon, Anna," she answered quietly. There was mockery in Anna's tone. What had she done, Sophie wondered, what new victory had she made?

"Dora drove me to the Gardiners," Anna announced, unpinning the hat. "She wanted to see the doctor about her rheumatism."

"I must go," said Sophie. Had she changed color under Anna's eyes, she wondered?

"The doctor had just heard from Jerome," pursued Anna, with a sidelong smile at Sophie. "He's been in New York on business, he said, but I suppose it was some woman."

"Very likely," said Grandmother Truelove. "That would be like Ezra."

"But this is Jerome," said Sophie. Her voice choked because she had not meant to speak.

"All the same," retorted the old woman. "The Gardiner men are all alike."

Sophie went over to the hall closet and put on her coat. She wanted to defy them both, to cry out that Jerome was as different from all the other Gardiners as she was different from all the other Trueloves. She wanted to say, "Jerome Gardiner loves only one woman and that woman is . . ." oh, she dared not say it, even to herself, even though she knew that it was true!

Anna watched her and was irritated at her composure. She sat down in the low chair Sophie had just left. It was hers now—she always sat there. Sophie's room was hers. Sophie was an outsider now. Anna wanted her to stay and see how completely she herself belonged. But Sophie was putting on her hat. Cecily came in. ("Oh dear, is she back?" Anna heard her whisper to Sophie.) She got out her workbasket and pretended not to see the two women whispering together, leaving her out. Presently Grandmother Truelove grasped both arms of her chair.

"I think I will go to the kitchen," she said. "It's warmer."

Anna made a move to help her but the old woman brushed her aside.

"Sophie will help me," she said.

Anna threaded her needle, while the three Truelove women went into the kitchen together. They wanted to crowd her out, those three women, but it would be they and not Anna Stacey who would be pushed out. She was inside now, no matter if they pretended she was an alien. Anna's fingers clenched over her needle. Interlopers before this had crowded out proud owners. And a woman—even a small, plain, weak woman—was born with the gift of being cruel. When Sophie came back in, Anna looked up from her sewing and smiled.

"Did Lynn tell you I saw him in town this morning?" she inquired, and added, fumbling casually for a spool of thread. "We had a chat, a nice, long chat."

"No," said Sophie. "He didn't tell me."

If Lynn, who did not like Anna, had finally listened to her, what could it have been that held him? Sophie's hand crept to her throat—had Anna told Lynn? Anna's eyes were lowered demurely over her embroidery, but a furtive smile twisted her lips. Sophie opened the door and went out to the buggy. John was impatiently flicking the whip over the snow.

"In a hurry?" inquired John. "The lower road is rougher but it's quicker."

What did it matter, Sophie thought dully, whether one drove slowly or swiftly to one's doom? Lynn would be there waiting for her, and the thing that Anna Stacey had told him would shine accusingly from his eyes.

A clock on the highboy ticked, its sound winked through hush, through night. Blackness sprawled over the bedroom, sucked walls, chairs and corners, challenged mirrors.

One o'clock—two o'clock—Sophie lay still and wondered if Lynn were asleep. How much had Anna told him or had she after all told him nothing? He had been no different when she came home last evening, and in her relief she had been almost hysterically demonstrative. Perhaps Anna had said nothing. "We had a long chat," she had said. That signified nothing. They might have talked of crops or weather or the family or a dozen things. Yet— and here Sophie's fingers tightened over her palms—Lynn had not spoken of seeing Anna in town. What did that mean? He had not mentioned her name, almost avoided it, you might say. Why?

"He's thinking of what to do about it," Sophie thought. "He knows, but he doesn't want to act right away."

Lying there beside her planning what must be done with his unfaithful wife. In the morning he would accuse her. She loved him and she had betrayed him. Sophie's heart knotted. Tick-tick in the darkness. In the morning—morning was hours away. She could not lie here beside him, not knowing what was in his head. Waiting was torture. She could die of it.

"Lynn," she whispered.

He did not answer. She put her hand on his shoulder. How could he sleep knowing—or did he know?

"Lynn . . ."

He lifted his head from the pillow.

"I wanted to ask you—" she must say it, she must!—"if you saw George or Anna in town."

Lynn stretched himself.

"No," he yawned. "Why?"

He knew about Jerome, she thought, he certainly knew, else why should he lie about having seen Anna?

"I—I only wondered," she choked.

"Nothing to lose sleep about, is it?" he inquired drowsily. Wasn't there something odd in his inflection, something suspiciously ironic? Now he was asleep again—or was he only feigning? Sophie flung her arm across her mouth to press back a moan of desperation. What had Anna told him, and why had he lied about seeing her? Sophie lay rigidly beside her husband, staring up into blackness, watching it centuries later change into the gray of morning.

Days passed and never once did Lynn speak Jerome Gardiner's name. Night after night went by with Sophie lying sleepless in bed, wondering if Anna had told Lynn. Why did he not speak out? Why didn't he accuse her? Anything but this endless uncertainty, finding double meanings in his most trivial comments, avoiding his eyes lest he read her confession in her own, starting up whenever he came in the house unexpectedly.

"Now he will say it," she would think. "Now he will ask me if it is true."

She prayed that Jerome would not come back. If he came she knew that she would go to him again, even with Lynn knowing. She could not stay away—she was tragically certain—even if Lynn were to follow her and accuse her. She would go knowing that each step sent her more surely to hell, knowing that her goal was not happiness but black destruction. He must stay away, that dark man, for his return would assuredly condemn her. Anna Stacey would say to Lynn, "Tonight we will follow them. See if what I told you is true." She would run, stumbling, down the dark road, across the bridge, and Lynn would be skulking behind her all the while.

"Oh, my dear," she would cry to him despairingly. "Can't you see I must go—I must? Don't follow me, I beg you. I mustn't hurt you because it's you I love. Go back to the white house and be sure of me. Know that I love you and forgive me for what I must do, because I can not turn back now, don't you understand?"

Anna Stacey's scornful knowing eyes would peer then from behind a bush, and Sophie's hands would go out pleadingly to her.

"Pity me, Anna. Pity me because I cannot turn back now. Pity me because I have left the man I love to go to the one I cannot deny. Pity me, Anna."

Thinking of him, Sophie's breath would come faster and she knew that she wanted Jerome again even in her danger. But he did not come back. She saw him behind Anna's mocking face when she went to her mother's house, but Anna did not mention him again. Only her lip curled when she looked at Sophie, because both of them knew that one was completely in the other's power. Sophie found this continual tension unbearable, and one day she went to the farm, pale from her sleepless nights, grimly determined to find out if Anna had told Lynn.

"I will ask her outright," Sophie promised herself. "This might go on for years and I would never know how much he knew or what she might tell him."

She found Anna upstairs in the children's room, reading to them. Cecily had found this means of getting Anna out of her path for a little while, and since the reading hour was as annoying to the children as it was to Anna, Cecily herself was the only one who profited by it. Sophie stood outside the doorway for a moment, striving for courage to face the other woman. Downstairs her mother had exclaimed:

"Sophie, you are ill! Just look at the shadows under your eyes! There isn't a bit of color in your face and your eyes look feverish. What is the matter? You should be in bed."

Sophie had tried to dismiss her mother's fears, but she knew then that Anna could see in her face her anxiety. She had wanted to seem indifferent, that was the only protection she could have.

Anna was sitting on a window ledge, reading from a big book in a bored monotonous voice. Custer, his thin dirty face tracked with recent tears, sat in a small red rocker and rocked sullenly. Lois and Vera were squeezed in the big bamboo rocker engaging in a private and sincere pinching bout. Occasionally one would emit a shriek, and Anna would stop short.

"If you don't want to hear the story of Persephone, I will tell your aunt and she'll send you back to Washington."

"No, no!" they would cry, and peace would reign for three solid minutes.

Sophie entered during one of these respites. Anna nodded to her and went on reading, but the children did not see her.

"As soon as she finishes I will send the children away and ask her," Sophie planned. "I will say, 'Anna, does Lynn know?' After all she can't hate me so much as to refuse to answer that. I'm not asking her to keep a secret, but only if she has told."

"After that Persephone had to live six months every year in purgatory," Anna read on.

Lois began to weep. "I don't like stories like that," she sniffed. "I never do like the stories you read and I hate this one."

"Oh, be still," Vera crushed her. "I like this story only I don't think it's fair Persephone had to go back to Pluto when it wasn't her fault at all."

"Oh yes it was," said Anna, and Sophie realized that she was looking at her with intent significance. "It was her fault. She knew what would happen if she ate the pomegranate. She knew perfectly well. There was no excuse for her. She got just what she deserved."

She closed the book sharply, her eyes smiling at Sophie, and there was neither pity nor kindness in them. Sophie met her glance gravely, unfalteringly. No, she would never ask for comfort from Anna Stacey.

"Cousin Sophie!" squealed Lois.

They pounced upon her and Sophie took Custer upon her lap.

"Did you come just to see us?" demanded Vera.

"Of course," answered Sophie, and did not turn her head as Anna slipped out the door.

A little while afterward coming down the staircase she fainted, and Bessie fanned her and said, leaning confidentially toward the distracted Cecily, "Don't you worry. She's probably going to have a baby, that's all. I know because I did the same thing myself the other day coming up the cellar steps."

After she had said it, Bessie guiltily clapped her hand over her mouth. She hadn't meant to tell. It was going to be a surprise, she had thought.

"She wanted to come with me," Cecily whispered to Sophie on Sunday afternoon in Sophie's kitchen. "I don't know why she insisted when she knows I don't like her."

"Where is she?" Sophie asked.

She put her hand to her forehead. There was no escaping Anna, she thought wearily.

Cecily pointed toward the barn.

"She said she wanted to see Lynn about something so she stopped out there, while George unhitched," she explained. "I was glad of it. I declare what with Lotta's young ones and George's wife around I never get a chance for a word with you."

Would Sophie tell her today about her baby, she wondered? You would think she'd tell her own mother as soon as she had any inkling, but Sophie was like that. Like the Trueloves. Kept their heads up and never spoke of the things closest to them.

Sophie kept her eyes fixed on the window. She could see George now, talking to Will Carter, but where was Anna, and where was Lynn? Were they whispering about her?

". . . but Bessie has always been such a good girl," her mother's voice was saying, "I just won't believe it of her, though she herself said—Lucy Anderson always was a gossip and Sara's just as bad. . . ."

Sophie nodded to her mother comprehendingly. Why didn't Anna come in the house? Why did Lynn, who loved her, listen to Anna? What were they saying to each other about her while George and Will Carter put the horse in the stall?

". . . would be different if she'd had no chance to marry but we all know John's wanted her ever since she's been with us, so there's really no reason. . . ."

Sophie's eyes grew brighter and she murmured, "Of course, Mother. No reason at all."

Ten minutes at least Anna had been out there talking to him. And George stood there stupidly talking to Will Carter. Why didn't he interrupt them? Why didn't he tell her to go in the house where women belonged?

". . . as if there hadn't been enough trouble under our roof in the last year—" her mother was crying now, and Sophie vaguely wondered why—"without Bessie—oh, it's too shameful. I won't believe it. Even from Bessie's own lips."

The kitchen trembled and the shiny black stove grew tall, blurred into the stovepipe. Sophie gripped the back of a chair until the dizziness passed. She must not faint again.

"I think I'll go out and tell them to come," she said thickly. "I need air."

"You have a headache?" anxiously asked Cecily. "Or is it something else, dear? Maybe I shouldn't have told you. Stephen said I shouldn't, but I had to talk it over with someone."

Sophie pushed open the kitchen door and stepped out. The air glittered with dry snow and the rush of cold air made her gasp but it braced her. She walked swiftly out to the carriage barn where Lynn was fussing with the new side curtains of the phaeton. Beside him was Anna, her muff up to her mouth, talking. Sophie drew in a breath and leaned back against the door. Anna was telling him now, there was no longer any doubt. She heard the words, "Bessie"—"lover"—and then—"graveyard" . . .

". . . but even she won't know who its father is."

"That's not true," Sophie heard words in a curious husky strained voice torn from her throat. "It's your child, Lynn. No matter what she says. I do know."

What had she said? She saw Anna's muff drop and saw Lynn's face turn gray, his blue eyes widen. She closed her eyes.

"I've been wicked," she said patiently, wearily, "I've been a bad wife, Lynn, as she says, but it will be our baby. Oh, I know that."

Lynn's hands were like steel on her wrists. Anna was suddenly scurrying toward the house, her little white face twisted over her shoulder in a half-terrified, half-triumphant backward glance.

"I don't know what you're talking about, Sophie," Lynn said in a slow, careful tone. "But I think it's time I did, don't you?"

They sat on either side of the table with the blue lamp between them lighting up Lynn's stern ashen face and then Sophie, spent, hollow-eyed, on the other side. Long, long ago Cecily and Anna had gone home. In the hours since these two had said the same words over and over, but at midnight they were still appalled at the ghastly thing between them.

"I don't know what to do," Lynn groaned finally, his head in his hands. "I can't live without you, Sophie. No man who ever loved you could ever be happy without you, or with anyone else. But I can't stand knowing that it might happen again. Any time. There might even be others "

"No," Sophie gasped. But did she know? Could one be sure of anything, in this world?

"If you could stop thinking of him . . ." Lynn got up and began walking up and down, "It's that more than anything. Knowing that he's in your mind . . ."

"I couldn't stop thinking," Sophie's voice was barely a whisper. "I couldn't promise that. You see I—I don't know. There are things that just happen to you, like rain or frost. You can't help them. He was like that. And I'm afraid to say it won't happen again. I don't know that. I know I love you. . . ."

"It was most unfortunate," sighed Lucy. "Her mother said she dn't know how it had happened."

"Nonsense!" said Grandmother Truelove. "Nonsense."

"Doctor Gardiner said it was an accident," said Cecily. "I mean about Estella."

"Pooh!" Sara's feathers gently vibrated. "Doctor Gardiner would say that about Bessie too. I'm afraid the doctor is a little too lenient."

"Of course he's never claimed to be a religious man," agreed Cecily. She finished the hem and began fussing with the buttonholes. They had almost glanced by the subject of Bessie's misfortune. How could Bessie have done it? How could she? Almost—but of course such a thing was impossible—as if she wanted to!

"The doctor just laughed when we spoke of Bessie yesterday," Lucy said, "Going east every year has given him some eastern ideas, I'm afraid. We thought since he was taking care of Bessie he'd know who the father was."

"But he said—these were his very words—'That's something no one will ever know,'" said Sara. "He said—oh, he really was vulgar, wasn't he, Lucy?—'If it had been one of you, I would swear it was an immaculate conception—his very words—but being Bessie, I have doubts!' An immaculate conception!"

"That sounds like Ezra," said Grandmother Truelove.

"This is Jay, you know," Cecily reminded her. "Ezra was his father and Jerome is his son.

"I think he meant something horrid, dear," reflected Sara. "Almost insulting. I'm sure we only asked about Bessie because we've always been interested in all the Trueloves and Bessie's just like one of the family."

"No," said Cecily hastily, and jabbed the needle in her thumb. "No!"

"I thought you did love me," Lynn said miserably. He kept his eyes away from her. He could not look at her pale suffering face.

"I do love you," Sophie answered, tears welling deep in her heart. "He never touched that part somehow. I don't feel that I have wronged you because what belongs to him never belonged to you, and what belongs to you can never go anyplace else. It's hard to understand. . . ."

Lynn stretched his arms rigidly upward, his eyes shut.

"I can't hold you in my arms, Sophie, and know you're only part mine. I've got to be sure. Even if you never saw him again . . . God, Sophie, how would I know what was in your mind, what things you were remembering."

He dropped into his chair again.

"How could you know?" Sophie repeated drearily. "How could I know? Oh, Lynn I'm afraid I am a bad woman. Like Bessie."

Lynn shook his head mutely.

"I'll leave you. You wouldn't ever be happy with me not being sure," she went on dully, her head lowered over her interlacing fingers. "I could go somewhere. I don't know. Somewhere."

Lynn drew a hand over his eyes.

"I don't know which would be worse," he said haltingly. "Having you here, not knowing, or losing you. I couldn't bear that, Sophie, your going away from me now. . . ."

They looked at each other. Each wanted nothing in the world so much as the peace and surety of the other's arms, the consolation of each other's lips, but they did not move. Only their eyes clung beseechingly.

"I was afraid," Lynn said after a while. "Do you remember? At the very beginning I was afraid."

Sophie nodded and they were silent. Even now there were things that could not be said. After a while Sophie went upstairs, and sat all night by her window looking out, unseeingly, at stars and snow and white hills piled against the black sky. Downstairs

Lynn fell asleep in the chair with the blue china lamp sputtering beside him and Sophie's embroidery at his feet.

When Sophie went to her mother's a few days later the Anderson girls were there. They swooped upon her as she entered as though they already knew, she thought, and she was obliged to sit down with them.

"We really came to see our little Anna," said Sara. "Doesn't she brighten up the place though, Cecily? Almost like having Sophie with you, isn't it?"

"Sophie looks poorly," Lucy said, cocking her head thoughtfully to one side. "Don't you think so, Sara?"

Sara twisted her chair to get a better view of Sophie, who kept her eyes downcast, her white hands fumbling a ribbon at her belt.

"She does look bad," agreed Sara. "Very bad. Thin, too. You see it, don't you, Cecily? No, I don't know when I've seen Sophie look so bad."

The sisters exchanged a look of quiet pleasure.

"I always said the air on the Ridge wasn't good," said Grandmother Truelove. She resented the ache in her bosom at the sight of Sophie's pallor. She was too old to suffer for her children.

Cecily was hemming a denim apron for Vera. She knew the girls had come to discuss Bessie's downfall, and she was inwardly preparing a detached composure to wear during their inquisition. Let them ask. Let them talk. The presence of Anna Stacey under one's roof taught one perpetual wariness. Even if they should mention that name . . . Stephen had said, "It doesn't

matter, my dear. It doesn't matter in the leas been a curious coldness in his eyes when he sn his silences were crowded with ghosts.

"Anna is in town with George today," said Cec she won't be back in time to see you. John drove ther

Sara rocked comfortably. Beneath her wide gre a lock of vari-colored hair strayed down and lay d her dried yellow cheek. She brushed it back with girlish gesture.

"We'll come again," she assured Cecily. "We like t Did Bessie go to town, too? Poor Bessie."

"Poor Bessie!" echoed Sara. "Of course we all know."

"Everyone knows," added Lucy. She half-closed her ey leaned toward Sophie. "Of course you knew? . . ."

"Bessie in trouble . . ." whispered Sara. She cupped her gl hand about her mouth. "Going to have a baby, you kr Tirzah, the Coles' hired girl, told."

"What of it?" Grandmother Truelove exclaimed crossly. S wished they would all go away and leave her to her reassuring s lence. "Some women have babies and some don't."

"But you see Bessie's not married," hissed Lucy, and shook her head smilingly at Cecily. ("Old women don't understand these things," her look conveyed.) "Some say it's the barber's child and some say it's the Coles' hired man's."

"Bessie knew both," blushed Sara. "Not that anyone blames you, Cecily. I'm sure you never had a thought but that Bessie was a good girl."

"I was as sure of her as I was of Sophie," Cecily declared.

Sophie could not lift her eyes. She and Bessie.

"She was just a little misled," regretted Lucy. "Just like Estella. You remember, Sara, when Estella Cross went astray."

"She had a baby," said Sara in a suitably low voice. She was only married six months."

"Just Sophie's age and all," said Sara. "Almost twins, weren't they?"

"Just a month's difference in our ages," Sophie answered in a low voice.

"Terrible thing for a girl," said Lucy. "To get in trouble. Mind, we're not blaming you, Cecily. I'm sure you couldn't be expected to look after Bessie that way."

"It does seem odd you never knew. They say," here Sara blushed again commendably, "she really knew quite a few young men."

"Imagine not knowing whose child!" exclaimed Lucy.

Sophie's hands twisted in her lap. Her teeth caught at her lip and dug into it. She and Bessie! She and Bessie with their grave-yard lovers! They would not have babies when their time came but ghouls, gray slant-eyed ghouls with dark shame on their lips. She and Bessie!

"John used to be so fond of her, too," said Lucy, catching sight that minute of John coming up the path from the kitchen.

"Perhaps one of the men could be made to marry her," suggested Sara. "Perhaps Stephen could arrange it."

"Nonsense!" said Grandmother Truelove out of a gentle doze. "Nonsense, Sara!"

Sara and Lucy exchanged a look.

"I'm sure such things have happened," said Sara sweetly. "Estella Cross's father, they said, took a shotgun. . . ."

"Stop!" Sophie choked, springing up in desperation. "Stop talking about it. Stop, do you hear? I—I won't have it!"

She was in tears. The two spinsters' jaws dropped, and Cecily was wide-eyed at her cool aloof Sophie's hysteria.

"Why Sophie!" she exclaimed.

The side door opened and George and Anna came in, snow sprinkling their coats. Sophie gripped the back of a chair, and hurried blindly out to the kitchen. She did not look at Anna, though Anna kept her eyes steadily upon her.

"What's the matter?" blustered George, tossing his cap into the corner behind the woodbox. Anna deliberately unbuttoned her gloves and smiled patronizingly at the Andersons.

"Sophie was always so fond of Bessie," explained Cecily. "She just won't believe it of her. I'm afraid it has upset her a good deal more than we realize."

"Very likely," said Anna.

She moved smilingly through the room toward the hall.

"I'm going upstairs and take a nap," she said. She was a lady, now, and why shouldn't she lounge when she felt like it?

"Should I wake you at suppertime?" asked George.

Anna's eyes blazed contemptuously.

"Mind your own affairs," she snapped, and flounced out of the room.

George looked around sheepishly. "Anna's an awful tease," he stammered, and got out his cap again to go to the barn.

"Tease!" echoed Grandmother Truelove. "Tease!"

"She went right upstairs with scarcely a how do you do," breathed Sara, her cheeks a brick red. "Did you see that, Lucy? She hardly spoke to us."

"And you came especially to see her," Cecily reminded them.

"I think she's a very disagreeable woman," gasped Sara, her hat beginning to shake in sympathetic agitation. "I must say . . ."

"Her mother runs a boardinghouse," said Lucy. "Did you know that, Cecily?"

"She has miserable table manners," said Sara. "Her great-grandmother on her mother's side couldn't speak a word of English."

"Foreigners," breathed Lucy.

They collected their woolen mufflers, jackets, capes, mittens, and in humiliated indignant silence made their way through the kitchen (for the drying galoshes) toward the door. Sophie was sitting at the kitchen table, her head leaning on her arm. John was behind the stove, warming his hands.

The two women modestly adjusted their rubbers.

"Are you still upset, Sophie?" Cecily asked anxiously.

Sophie shook her head and smiled.

"I was just telling Sophie that Bessie and I have decided to hitch up," said John proudly. "You know Bessie's been awful mean to me for a long time, but I guess I showed her a thing or two. She can't keep that up with a man like me. Not by a damned sight. When she started in being smart this morning at breakfast I just told her a thing or two and I put her right in her place. I guess I'm master now all right."

"You're marrying her?" chorused Lucy and Sara.

John nodded triumphantly.

"You bet your life I am," he boasted. "When I go after a woman, I get her, by cracky, and no nonsense about it. It took ten years to do it, but by gee, I got her in the end, didn't I?"

"That's splendid," said Lucy and followed her sister out to the sleigh without another word.

"I'm a man what gets what he goes after," floated arrogantly after them.

Sophie saw them go with almost hysterical relief. But Anna Stacey was still in the house. Anna, whose eyes said, "You and Bessie! You and Bessie!"

When Bessie came up from the cellar she put her hand familiarly on Sophie's shoulder.

"As if she knows we are alike," shuddered Sophie, and tried not to see the candid convexity of Bessie's apron.

For Sophie there was no peace in the white house by the woods, nor any consolation under her father's roof. Lynn's suffering eyes followed her wherever she went, and at the Truelove farm there was always Anna Stacey to subtly remind her of her kinship with Bessie.

In her own house dust filmed the furniture, monograms remained unworked on the wedding linen, and Sophie, unheeding, stood at her window staring at gray cold skies. Seven more months and she would have a child. Lynn's. But never in all this world would he be sure of that. Before she should open her eyes after the day of pain, she would think—hearing Doctor Gardiner's voice and the baby's first wail—"Oh God, let me die before I see Lynn's face. Let me die before I see the doubt in his eyes. . . ." But she would live and there would be Lynn, his head buried in his arms, suffering because he loved her and did not know that the child she had borne was his. . . . How could she go on endlessly torturing him? They could not speak of the thing between them, and it would grow as the child grew. It would be a doomed child, and the phantom of it's mother's shame would prowl after it, and she, the mother, would know and be helpless.

Once Lynn seized her with desperate intensity and kissed her as he had never kissed her before.

"It doesn't matter," he told her fiercely, "It doesn't matter, do you hear? You love me and you're mine. Mine—do you understand? No matter—" in spite of himself his arms loosened their hold and his voice trembled— "no matter who has loved you before, no matter . . ."

Sophie blinked away tears. It was no use. Everywhere she turned she ached for herself and for Lynn. It would be forever like this. And if some day Jerome Gardiner should return—Sophie's heart quickened. . . .

"Shame, shame," she told herself in horror, "you should be ashamed, but you are glad, Sophie Truelove. You can see Lynn's eyes and not be sorry about that other man. You can be insulted by Anna Stacey's mockery and yet be glad—glad that once you were blown by a wind from hell. You can weep for one man's unhappiness and in your heart want to torture him again, because if he—that other man—called to you, you would go!"

If there were a way of getting letters from Jerome—if there were some way of hearing from him, of seeing in his bold hand-

writing the words he had said to her when she was in his arms. . . . Now she might never see him again. She should be glad of that for his absence protected her. But in the confusion of her desires the thought of Jerome alone was savagely clear-cut, the moments with him the only ones in all her life that had been simple. If she should see him again, she knew the tangle in her brain would give way before one radiant overwhelming need, one blind uncomplicated emotion that swept aside all doubts, all hesitation, all remorse.

"But I shall not see him," she thought. "I must not hurt Lynn anymore."

Her father came in on his way from town to show her a letter that had come from Lotta. While he read it Sophie pondered, "What showed Aunt Lotta her way out? How do people find out what to do? I can't take the way Mary Cecily did. I can't go away as Aunt Lotta did. Perhaps if I could see Jerome . . ." Thoughts were cruel, brutal things that left one staggered at one's own self-ishness. . . . If she could see Jerome!

"You see Lotta wants the children," Stephen said, folding the letter. "I don't like the idea of their leaving your mother now that she's fond of them, but there's nothing else to be done."

"Mother will miss them," Sophie said abstractedly.

"Well, Lotta's not at all strong," Stephen said. "She seems to be having trouble of some sort, and you'll find out when you have children of your own, Sophie, that they comfort you when you're low. Your mother will tell you that."

Sophie's fingers tapped the arm of her chair. Her eyes were on a faraway hill. She was breathless before the thought that was slowly lettering her brain. Her embroidery dropped from her lap while her father stood leaning against the mantel smoking reflectively.

"Lotta is a very lonely woman," he mused. "No one ever un-derstood her and she won't be like other people. Always kept things to herself, the way you are, my dear. . . . I used to think she might be good for you in her odd way. You've led a pretty commonplace life. Never traveled. Never left home."

"Yes," Sophie agreed. "I've never been to any city."

"A commonplace life," repeated her father. "Lotta wrote once that we ought to send you to a seminary in Washington."

"I remember that," said Sophie, her eyes resting thoughtfully on her father. "But I had never gone anyplace alone. I wonder if I should be afraid now."

"No need now," smiled Stephen. "Lynn will always take care of you."

Sophie twisted her wedding ring slowly.

"But if I should have to go alone sometime," she murmured, "I wonder if I could . . ."

Stephen tapped his pipe on the ash bowl and buttoned up his coat.

"I guess you won't be going anywhere alone," he said comfortably. "I guess not. Well, I must be getting home and tell your mother about the children leaving."

"When will they go?" asked Sophie.

"Next month," answered Stephen. "I'll take them over to the station at the Ridge. The ten o'clock train will stop if there are passengers. Lands them in Washington on the next evening."

"I wish I could take them," she said half to herself.

Her father pinched her cheek.

"What? You've traveled less than even Custer!"

He put on his coat and great woolen mittens.

"Too bad you can't come over with me," he said. "Your mother thinks you stay away because of Bessie."

"Oh no," said Sophie a little faintly.

Her father looked down at her gravely.

"I hoped not," he said. "Bessie couldn't help it. All of us have things happen to us that we can't help, things sometime that change a whole life."

"I know," nodded Sophie and watched her father make his way through the snowy path out to his sleigh. He waved to her and she waved back. Her other hand was at her throat—throbbing, throbbing with the excitement of a vague immense thought, a thought as terrifying and as tremendous as the door of heaven.

Night, muffled and star-stabbed, waited for her. The snowy road waited for her, waited for her carriage tracks as if it had always known she would come this way. Through the dark tree-arched road her horse trotted, stepping on crackling twigs and skeletons of dead bushes. Sophie had never held the reins before and her hands trembled with their responsibility, and with fear of the thing she was doing. Ten o'clock, her father had said, at ten o'clock the train went to Washington. Surely she would turn back before she came to the bend in the road, surely she would not go on. She drew in the reins involuntarily, and the mare slowed her pace. The wind blew her veil against her eyes. She was cold. She should have worn a woolen scarf. Now she could not control her shivering. She might turn back now . . . (Lynn's hurt eyes, growing old with doubt frozen in his heart, Anna Stacey's knowing, scornful eyes, herself alone with her shamed memories. . . .) Sophie clucked and the mare went ahead.

Ridiculous to have taken this road when it was the one the men would take coming home from town meeting. Supposing she should meet them—they might have left earlier than usual, it might have been a short meeting!—They would recognize the mare at once and stop.

"I was just taking a little drive," she would stammer.

Absurd! She, who had never held the reins before. She would not forget her panic in the dark stable, the heavy heap of leather harnesses, the bewildering tangle of reins, the halter—she could never unravel them, she thought. And then the mare quietly, tactfully nosing each piece as it should be put on, waiting impervious to her gasping commands until she had adjusted an overlooked buckle with shaking, unaccustomed fingers. Not until she was actually in the seat did she admit the enormous truth. She was running away. She had not said it to herself even at supper when Lynn asked her why she wore her velveteen dress.

"I'm cold," she said. "It's the only dress that really keeps me warm."

When George stopped to take him in to the meeting as he did each Wednesday, she kissed Lynn good-bye. How conscious they were of their caresses now, he thinking of another who had known her lips, and she knowing his thoughts. Then she went upstairs. Even when she pulled the portmanteau from the closet she did not admit her plan, even while she was packing it in methodic considered haste. Only her heart beat very fast and she saw herself in the mirror deathly white with tight lips and shining eyes. But in the buggy she whispered:

"I am running away. I will never see him again or her eyes. They cannot reproach me. I shall not wonder what is in their minds, or what people know, what they are saying. I shan't see Bessie and know that I am like her. No one can say it. I shan't read it in their eyes. . . .

Far away a train whistle sounded. Sophie had passed the bend in the road and knew she would not meet the men returning. She was taking the upper road—past the Andersons (there was no light)—and now past the white staring graveyard with a wind shrieking over it, tearing the snow from the monuments. Here was her tomb, Sophie saw, and instinctively flicked the reins, her lips parted, her breath coming fast. She would see him. She would see him again. . . . The road reached its highest point and trees sloped down on either side into the valley. Across the valley on the opposite hill her own house came into view for an instant. She leaned out and an exhausting loneliness overwhelmed her. The white house with the green shutters was as empty as a sky. It was jeweled with light, and she remembered that she had left with all the lamps burning proudly, as though there were no darkness or desolation inside. They glittered now across the valley, gaudily, emptily, lights from a cold white house with green shutters. . . . It was far far away that white house, and that grave fair man was far, far away, so far that Sophie could not see his eyes. He was only a blue-white radiance behind the hill that as she rode along obscured the house. A blue-white radiance. . . . Now the lights of the station below, the whistle of a train, and then a dark rich excitement reached out to her, drew her into itself. She was going to see him again, going to see Jerome Gardiner.

When would he come, Sophie wondered?

Here in the same city with him she marveled that she could have kept from him for so long. What incredible power after that night in the graveyard could have held her, what thing was strong enough after that night in the hut to have kept her from going to him? Here in Lotta's dark, velvet-muffled drawing room the Truelove acres were a tiny diminishing imprint, the hands out entreating her to be sane now that her letter trembled in their grasp had no power to move her, her father's voice was a far-off echo, her mother's face with stabbed hurt eyes a fading medallion. The love of Lynn Hamilton and Sophie Truelove was in her curiously numb mind only a faint legend, a sad bell chiming in an historic belfry. Here, looking from the balcony window across the park, the sense of Lotta's presence about her, Sophie could not reconstruct the old terror, the monstrous shadows threatening her in Anna's eyes or swaying in a tree at night. She could think of Lynn's blue sorrowing eyes and say with strange detachment, "What a pity that someone should hurt him! It was not I who did but another Sophie. What a pity that he should suffer."

When would Jerome come? She had wanted to tell Lotta everything, to beg her to find what the stars decreed for her, but in the days she had been here, there had been sufficient comfort in Lotta's sheer propinquity, the sense of her tacit understanding. Lotta knew, Sophie thought. Inside the Ephemeris volume was a little marker in Lotta's writing, July 1, 1876, Sophie's birthday, and Sophie knew that someday Lotta would plot with circles and charts and she would know then what had been and what was to be.

When would he come? What would he say? What could they plan? He had a wife. She, Sophie, had only been one of his women, Anna Stacey and Grandmother Truelove had implied. But she knew this was not just. Perhaps there had been others, but the thing that existed between them could not be like the others.

Wandering now about the drawing room, her hand resting on gilded chair backs, on a brocaded wall, Sophie could think of that night on the tombstone as a beautiful, grave, precious thing, and now there was no shame.

When would he come?

She had written to him only one line. Behind her in the hall Lotta's Hindu servant moved about. Upstairs in Lotta's chamber, Lotta sat at a low table by the balcony window, her blonde head bent over papers and worn reference books. A brilliant blue velvet robe was caught about her and enhanced the pallor of her face, the olive shadows under her eyes. Above a roughly penciled chart was written, "Sophie Truelove, b. midnight July 1, 1876, Ashton, Ohio." Lotta could remember when the air had shuddered with the approach of things . . . a faint tingling in the tips of her limp fingers . . . her head heavy with slow-revealing apocryphal murals . . . about her the atmosphere weighted with presences, and in her veins a rare singing peace, a certainty of what would be. . . . In her fingertips she held a lost magic, a pale ecstasy that stripped her of all weight, all body, and left her as light, as perfect as a flame. About her crowded dim presences, breathing shadows, and one exquisitely sad wraith in an ancient headdress, her flowing veil masking her lips. Lotta knew those slanting eyes and thought of Adam Trygloe's bride.

"Sophie Truelove," she wrote, "born at midnight, July . . ."

When—when would he come, Sophie wondered. . . . She wanted to sit at the window from morning till night, watching for him, but that would not bring him. She wanted to rush to the hall whenever the doorbell rang but that would not hurry him. There would come a moment, she thought, when waiting would suddenly be intolerable as it was the night she had first gone to meet him. . . . Now beveled gold mirrors along the wall, above the mantel, between the windows, exchanged images of a slender woman in black velvet with blue-black hair, gave each other a white profile, a flash of black-fringed eyes, and then her back as she faced abruptly a man in the doorway. . .

It seemed to Sophie, seeing Jerome Gardiner again, that what she had done was the only thing possible to her. They moved toward each other swiftly and at the touch of her hand Jerome's went to his eyes as if once again to shut out an unendurable radiance. There was the old panic when their lips met, the retreat of all words or necessity for them. . . . Sophie drew back a little.

"You see," she said—to have said his name aloud would have been too shamelessly caressing!—"I had to come to you at last . . .

it was only to see you this once. I shall live here with Aunt Lotta
until . . . but I had to come. There were so many things . . ."

It was unbelievable that a man she had seen so few times,
whose face she could not clearly remember, should have such absolute power over her, should be able by his sheer presence to
bring her such burning peace. . . . He would not allow her to
draw away.

"I've never stopped thinking of you, Sophie," he said almost
wearily. "Things had to happen to us—I knew it from the first—
even that market day in Ashton when I saw you for the first time.
We knew, then, didn't we?"

Their cheeks were pressed against each other's. She had wanted
to be sane and cool—there were so many things to be planned—
but the blood was dancing in her head and she knew only the necessity of their being together. It would always be this way. There
was no calm or safety with this man. Always he would be the dark
stranger, carrying her into night and danger. Back in her white
house the thought of this perilous love would have drawn her in-
evitably to him. One day or another she would have had to come
to him, hypnotized, unswervingly to his arms.

"You'll come with me, of course," Jerome said after she had
told him, "I must arrange for that."

She nodded slowly. She sat twisting the wedding ring on her
finger.

"It will be Lynn's child," she said.

"I know," he answered, "but my Sophie."

She saw them in a little house outside the city. Outcast really, for
divorces were slow matters. He would be kind, always, and exquisitely tender, because there was in him the same tragic uncertainty of
self that she herself knew. The thing that made him rich in understanding, Sophie suddenly thought, was the awareness of his own
weakness. Weak. The Gardiner men were weak with women. The
Gardiner men were always weak with women. Jerome and Jay,

and Ezra before them. Weak . . . Sophie's eyes widened with sick misgiving. If . . . if . . . She saw herself waiting for him to come to her in their house, and he—walking through a park with someone else. . . . She remembered Senator Anderson's wife.

"Will there be others," she was thinking aloud, "other Sophies?"

Jerome took her face in his two hands, his eyes deep in her's.

"It's you I love, Sophie," he said savagely, "After you there couldn't be anyone else. . . . You know that."

Sophie shook her head.

"No," she said, "I don't know. It's so hard to know. We can't ever be sure, can we, dear?"

"There shall be no one else," he repeated.

But when their lips met again Sophie closed her eyes that she should not see the veiled fear in his.

Lying in Jerome's arms, Sophie knew that this was her destiny. Peace was in a white hushed house with Lynn, but for her there must be ecstasy and torment. How far away she was from Lynn now . . . (Alone in the house he had built for his bride, his lips tight, refusing the jubilant sympathy in Anna Stacey's eyes, avoiding the face in the daguerreotype over the organ, his eyes blue as cobalt and hard with what he had learned now of love.)

Sophie, her cheek against her lover's throat, her body throbbing in his arms, knew that he would hurt her as she had hurt Lynn, and that he would hold her forever because of his power to make her suffer. There would be moments—this she knew—when she would want only Lynn to shield her, to console her for Jerome's wounds. A woman needed two lovers, one to comfort her for the torment the other caused her.

What would happen when her child was born, Sophie wondered? In the dark of the chamber she sensed Jerome all about her. His massive dresser over there, the rectangle of dim light that was the door to his study-book-lined walls, English riding prints, photographs of his favorite horses, a fog of cigar smoke in the air. She was glad his wife had never stayed here. In six months, after the baby came, they two could be together always instead of these occasional hours. . . . A little house on the edge of the city, Jerome said. . . . He never wanted to open the house where he and Lucille had lived. . . . A little house on the edge of the city as soon as their marriage would be arranged.

Sophie's hand touched his face in the darkness. The wet night in the graveyard was far removed, yet contact still brought back that blind whirling confusion. How soon would her family know everything, she wondered? And Lynn. . . .

Jerome, sleeping, made a little sound. It was Sophie, Sophie he held in his arms, not Zelda, nor Lisa, nor Mary . . . Sophie, the infinitely desirable, the always unconquerable. Now she was his, as she was meant to be, she was the woman he had sought in all other women, but he could feel her slipping from him, and it was a yellow head on his shoulder. Zelda . . . God, this was unbearable that the height of his desire should be confused with the heights of other desires. Sophie, it was, slim, hauntingly lovely, in the bedroom doorway in candle glow, and there was the quick crossing of their desires; Sophie, running toward him in the darkness, and the two of them lashed by a wind down the black road; Sophie here at last in his own arms . . . and now there could be no one else, for here was the perfection for which he had been fumbling. Yet somehow it seemed to him a forest at dawn, and they were lying under a tree, and all this was new, and he was shaking with the cold dew and an agony of fear. Then the two thin arms held out to him, and Stella, the Bad Girl, singing out, "Are you sorry—are you afraid now?"

(Sophie—Sophie—he hunted through the fog of sleep for her.)

"No," he had denied and shuddered again. It was the cold dew and not terror—oh surely he was not afraid of this tremendous truth he had just learned, surely he was not afraid. . . .

He blinked resolutely. Sophie. It was Sophie and there would never be anyone else. Not Stella nor Lisa nor Zelda nor Mary . . . Sophie . . . His eyelids drooped again. Drowsily his lips touched her hair and he was happy. Now their dreams merged into each other's and Jerome saw an old woman in a wicker armchair and heard her say, "Weak with women. Weak." And Sophie saw a blonde woman with eyes like Mrs. Anderson's. In her sudden fear she saw herself running down a dark country road that had long been waiting for her footsteps, toward a white house, lamps flaring defiantly in every window . . . and whispering, "Lynn . . . Lynn . . ."

A NOTE ON THE AUTHOR

DAWN POWELL was born in Mt. Gilead, Ohio, in 1897. In
1918 she moved to New York City where she lived and
wrote until her death from cancer in 1965. She was the
author of fifteen novels, numerous short stories, and a
half dozen plays.

A NOTE ON THE BOOK

The text for this book was composed by Steerforth Press
using a digital version of Granjon, a typeface designed
by George W. Jones and first issued by Linotype in 1928. All
Steerforth books are printed on acid free papers and this
book was bound by BookCrafters of Chelsea, Michigan.

Also by Dawn Powell

ANGELS ON TOAST

COME BACK TO SORRENTO

DANCE NIGHT

THE GOLDEN SPUR

THE HAPPY ISLAND

THE LOCUSTS HAVE NO KING

MY HOME IS FAR AWAY

A TIME TO BE BORN

TURN, MAGIC WHEEL

THE WICKED PAVILION

THE DIARIES OF DAWN POWELL: 1931–1965

DAWN POWELL AT HER BEST
Including the novels DANCE NIGHT
and TURN, MAGIC WHEEL and selected stories